———————— ★ ————————

A thin, but deep cut had been made on her throat, and the blood oozing from the wound was soaking the riding jacket with its matching color. Blood also dripped from her mouth, leaving stains on both sides of her lips. What was apparently Ms. Carlisle's wristwatch had been removed and placed across her chest. Its face had been smashed.

Wilson felt a surge of nausea, which was suddenly held in check by curiosity. Amid the redness, he saw a glint of silver. He looked closer at Ms. Carlisle's mouth. As he peered at her open lips, he saw that between her teeth, almost ready to fall out, was a shiny coin.

———————— ★ ————————

A LESSON IN
MURDER

AUGUSTUS CILEONE

W❂RLDWIDE®

TORONTO • NEW YORK • LONDON
AMSTERDAM • PARIS • SYDNEY • HAMBURG
STOCKHOLM • ATHENS • TOKYO • MILAN
MADRID • WARSAW • BUDAPEST • AUCKLAND

Recycling programs
for this product may
not exist in your area.

A LESSON IN MURDER

A Worldwide Mystery/November 2009

First published by Oak Tree Press.

ISBN-13: 978-0-373-26691-3

Printed in U.S.A.

For Jessica, my best friend and
a wonderful daughter

ONE

THE CAR WAS THERE, as usual. Not that it was always the same car that George Wheeler drove three days a week from his luxurious Chestnut Hill house in Philadelphia to the secluded Valley Green section of Fairmount Park. On Mondays, he drove his Mercedes, on Wednesdays, he used the Jaguar, and on Fridays, he took his BMW. So, on this rather warm early May Monday, at 7:00 a.m., Jason Barnum noted the hearse-black Mercedes parked in the usual spot.

Wheeler was usually there at 6:30 a.m., warming up his fifty-six-year-old body with a short jog, and would return to his car to wait for Barnum, who would walk from his car, parked a mile away. They would then run together and eventually return to Barnum's car. Barnum would then give Wheeler a lift back to his car. Barnum would have preferred that these jogs contained more pleasure than business. But, Barnum's company provided the advertising campaigns for Wheeler's lucrative pharmaceutical business, and Wheeler always wanted to pitch ideas at Barnum while they ran.

As he walked toward the shiny new Mercedes, Barnum admired it, but realized it was not as impressive as many of the automobiles in Wheeler's collection of antique cars, which were never used for mere transportation. Wheeler kept those for show to impress a new client with the sweet tangible smell of success.

The car was there, but where was Wheeler? Maybe he was taking it slow getting back, given the high morning temperature. However, Barnum could not recall Wheeler ever being anything but punctual. He approached the car, and a tingle of apprehension spread quickly through Barnum. He thought he could see someone sitting behind the steering wheel. As he came closer to the car on the driver's rear side, he could make out Wheeler's full head of salt-and-pepper colored hair above the back of the front seat. His hands were on the steering wheel, as if in the act of driving. As Barnum reached the front door, he knew something was frightfully wrong. The safety belt harness secured Wheeler's body, but his head was tilted somewhat sideways, away from Barnum, on the headrest. Some semi-coagulated blood ran down the side of Wheeler's head. Barnum tensed his muscles, trying to harden himself against what he was about to see. He opened the car door to get a better look. He quickly drew back, sucking in air through his mouth. He forced himself to observe the scene again. He started breathing quickly, and walked backwards away from the car.

George Wheeler sat in the driver's seat, looking as lifeless as the car in which he was sitting. On the seat next to him was a stuffed animal, which looked like Walt Disney's Pluto. A large, flat, hardback book lay open in his lap. Wheeler's usual black horn-rimmed glasses had been replaced with large, bright yellow-framed spectacles. Barnum again peered in the window quickly. Wheeler's tan, healthy-looking face had been smeared with what appeared to be charcoal ashes.

TWO

"IT'S A MYSTERY," said Maxwell Hunter. He surveyed his last-period English class on Wednesday afternoon, not speaking again until he had everyone's attention.

"All of literature is a mystery. The writer is giving you clues in the words, the setting, the plot, the characters…and even in the style. He or she wants you to join in the fun of figuring out how all the pieces fit together." He paused and smiled.

"Each of us," he continued, "is Sherlock Holmes, whether it comes to art, or, for that matter, life. We're just trying to find out what's going on."

Hunter then turned to the blackboard where the poem was written.

The Second Coming

Turning and turning in the widening gyre
The falcon cannot hear the falconer;
Things fall apart; the center cannot hold;
Mere anarchy is loosed upon the world,
The blood-dimmed tide is loosed, and
    everywhere
The ceremony of innocence is drowned;
The best lack all conviction, while the worst
Are full of passionate intensity.
Surely some revelation is at hand;
Surely the Second Coming is at hand.
The Second Coming! Hardly are those
    words out
When a vast image out of Spiritus Mundi
Troubles my sight: somewhere in sands of
    the desert
A shape with lion body and the head of a
    man,
A gaze blank and pitiless as the sun,
Is moving its slow thighs, while all about it
Reel shadows of the indignant desert birds.
The darkness drops again; but now I know
That twenty centuries of stony sleep

Were vexed to nightmare by a rocking cradle,
And what rough beast, its hour come round
*   at last,*
Slouches towards Bethlehem to be born?

" 'Turning and turning in the widening gyre,' "
said Hunter, moving his hands as if stirring a big
pot as he spoke the words.

"Yeats wants you to feel the 'turning.' You have
to open your mouth wide to say 'widening.' He
wants you to feel things loosening up."

"'Things fall apart,'" he read. "Even in his
meter, Yeats is reinforcing his meaning. The first
two words have strong accents, but then you get
to 'apart,' and you have an unstressed syllable—
a weakening, a breaking away, because there is no
longer a 'center' to hold 'Things' together."

Hunter looked hard at his class.

"Yeats saw us moving away from the spiritual
toward the worship of things as we headed toward
the future, when we will see that 'The blood-
dimmed tide is loosed, and everywhere/The
ceremony of innocence is drowned.'"

James Learner sat at the back of the class and
thought about how much Hunter enjoyed doing

the literary detective bit. Learner had been in Hunter's eleventh grade class, and had decided to do independent study with him during the spring semester of Learner's last year at Eastern Friends School. He was sitting in on a few English classes that interested him, and which he felt would help him when he attended the University of Pennsylvania in the fall.

Learner had known Hunter for as long as he could remember. Their parents had been neighbors in the Philadelphia suburb of Whitemarsh. Hunter's parents had been teachers back then, and had since retired. Both of Learner's parents were lawyers. Hunter had baby-sat Learner when James was a very young child. Learner remembered Hunter reading to him from picture books and fairy tale collections. At that time, Hunter no longer lived at his parents' home, but would visit often, staying over many times, and both families would have dinner together. Later, the children's stories were replaced by Hunter's tales of going to college in the late 1960's and early 1970's, with descriptions of protests and conflicts between the youth of that time and the establishment. The Learners moved away, to a housing development in Upper Bucks County, and James had attended the public schools there. He lost touch with Hunter, until James' parents decided that their son would have a better chance of going to a prestigious college if he graduated from a private school. When they learned that Hunter had been teaching at Eastern Friends School, they looked up their old neighbor. After they checked out the school, the family agreed that James should transfer to EFS.

Learner looked at Hunter, as the class continued, and saw how the teacher contrasted in appearance with the boys in the class. He wore the Sixties legacy look: shaggy hair; round, steel-rimmed glasses; wrangler shirt; and faded jeans. The boys, including himself, had various shaved haircuts, ranging from bald to military crew cut. But the clothes were either expensive preppy, or athletic, except for the students who came from the less financially endowed families.

Hunter drove an old Volkswagen. Despite its being the "people's car," Learner would kid Hunter about how the teacher was driving a Nazi automobile. Hunter said the two of them should form an alliance, since Learner drove a Mazda

Miata. That was one thing Learner liked about Hunter—the man never took himself too seriously.

Hunter continued to address Yeats' themes of the spiritual and the material, and of art and life, making references to "Leda and the Swan" and the Byzantium poems.

"Yeats sought the balance between two worlds," said Hunter. "I would like you to think about that for our next class, and come in with suggestions of your own on how we, today, can walk that tightrope between the worlds of the intangible and the real."

As the class ended, and the students emptied out of the classroom, Learner went up to Hunter's desk as the teacher packed away his books into a brown leather briefcase.

"You must have really enjoyed yourself today," kidded Learner, "using Yeats to sing your 'Goddamn the yuppie man' song."

"What are you talking about?" asked Hunter, with mock hurt in his voice. "Did I not present the great William Butler Yeats' poetry accurately?"

"Emphasis, Teach, emphasis. Nobody is

really objective. Everyone is always working his own angle."

Hunter knew James Learner was goading him, which was allowable because of their long friendship. But, there was a serious resigned cynicism underlying Learner's words that saddened Hunter.

"I have to move it," said Hunter. "Faculty meeting."

They walked down the steps to the first floor into the main entrance hall of the combined middle and upper schools. The walls were white stucco, trimmed with solid oak moldings. They passed the trophy cases, which were filled with pictures and awards, both scholastic and athletic, chronicling the school's three hundred year history. They passed through the large doors to the main entrance, which were painted yellow on the inside, and green on the outside. Carved in granite over the door on the outside was the school's motto: "Education—The Richest Possession."

As they walked across the spacious, green campus, situated in the exclusive Eastwood section of the city, toward the Quaker meetinghouse where the faculty session was to take place, Hunter looked at the almost completed Olympic-size indoor swimming pool. James noticed Hunter's gaze.

"Do you think the pool will be completed before graduation day?" Learner asked.

"It's supposed to be. Old Dr. Bergman set the deadline, and he's the one picking up the hefty portion of the tab," said Hunter.

"Yeah, it sure helps to have alumni with lots of bucks," said Learner.

Hunter turned to Learner.

"Are you going to be one of those alumni, James?" he asked.

"Well," mused Learner, "Mom and Dad would like me to be a lawyer, and join the firm. Sounds good. Why do you ask? Do you want me to become an English teacher?"

Hunter laughed.

"Well, it's true you won't be donating any pools on a teacher's salary," he said.

"Yeah," agreed Learner, and he added with a smile, "but at least you can work at a place where they have one, and are able to go for a swim sometimes for free."

There was a pause.

"Speaking of alumni," said Learner, "how about what happened to George Wheeler? Pretty scary, huh? He was still involved with the school, wasn't he?"

"Sure was," answered Hunter. "He funded large grants to the science department. He was also very influential in getting other successful alumni to donate substantial sums of money to EFS. He still liked going to most of the sporting events, also."

Hunter stopped.

"After reading the paper, I thought that it sure sounded as if the killer knew Wheeler was going to be at that spot in the park."

"Why?" asked James.

"Nothing of any value was taken. It wasn't just some random robbery," said Hunter.

Learner shrugged.

"Could just have been some nut," he said.

Hunter shook his head.

"I don't know," he said. "Newspaper said the police don't have any clues. No prints, no clothing fibers. There was no sign of a struggle, which would have left blood or saliva stains. If this one is a nut, he's going to be a tough one to crack.

There's supposed to be a police detective at the faculty meeting today asking some questions."

"Uh-oh!" laughed Learner. "Now don't go making pig sounds, oinking all over the place. These aren't those good old days of yours."

"I promise I'll be on my best behavior," said Hunter, but he had to admit to himself that he still had a hard time trusting cops.

As they approached Learner's Miata, they noticed Hank Jackson, an African-American student who was on the varsity basketball team with Learner. Jackson was admiring the black sports coup.

"Um, um!" he said. "Now this is a car. Take me for a ride sometime, James?"

"You got it, Hank. How about Friday after school, we go for some pizza. My treat," said Learner.

"OK, but I can pay my way," said Jackson. He started to jog away, his duffel bag flopping at his side. "I've got to catch a bus to get to my job. See you later."

Jackson cut across the large lawn toward the tennis courts next to the school entrance to the street.

"How's Jackson doing in his classes?" Hunter

asked Learner. He wanted a student's perspective as to how a minority student, who had been recruited because of his special talents, was making out. Learner was a good source since he was Jackson's friend.

"Not bad," said Learner. "Hank's a hard worker. He has a math tutor who's helping him with his algebra. Nine years of public school education do not exactly prepare someone for the academic stuff that this place throws at you."

Before Hunter had a chance to say good-bye to James, he heard a familiar voice calling from behind.

"I'll save you a seat at the meeting, Max, but, avanti!"

It was Patricia Delvecchio. Hunter watched her pretty form, and her dark brown hair bouncing behind, as she headed for the Quaker meetinghouse.

"So, how come you're so sweet on Miss Delvecchio?" asked James. "I know! She's a foreign-language teacher, you don't know what she's talking about, and, of course, as we know, you love a mystery, right?"

"Do the English words 'It's none of your

business' contain any meaning for you? Or, do you need a translator?" said Hunter.

He continued seriously.

"She grew up in Europe. She gives me a different viewpoint on work, people, and things in general. I find her…refreshingly non-American."

"Oooh! Sounds pretty subversive to me," kidded Learner.

There was a pause.

"I found more kids cheating. Tenth grade, third period. I can't get used to that," said Hunter.

Learner shrugged.

"Unfortunately," he said, "being dishonest has become the accepted thing to do. Some do it; more do it, and get away with it. People look around and see it all over. They can see it on CNN every day. Pretty soon, a kid feels like a dope if he doesn't give it a shot."

Hunter looked hard at James.

"Did you ever do it?" he asked Learner.

Learner smiled, and then looked away.

"Not in your class, I didn't. Besides, I found out I was so smart, I didn't need to cheat," he said with exaggerated arrogance. "Come on, Sixties rule-breaker man. Didn't you ever cheat, not even on one test, on one measly little quiz, huh?"

Hunter looked down, and spoke, sounding for some reason almost apologetic.

"No, as a matter of fact, I never did."

THREE

ONE PART OF Maxwell Hunter's mind tried to pay attention to the faculty meeting that was going on at the Eastern Friends School meetinghouse. However, the rest of his thoughts shifted to the warmth and passion he was feeling for Patricia, who was sitting next to him. And, just as quickly, his mind raced 180 degrees in the opposite direction as he observed, and contemplated, the large meetinghouse, and what it stood for.

Headmaster William Falls, Jr., was conducting the proceedings, and his soothing, but crisp words resonated and soared in the oak-beamed hall. Hunter, who was definitely not religious in any orthodox sense, liked the Quaker practice of meeting for worship. Students, from kindergarten through twelfth grade, met once a week in the meetinghouse. Faculty and administrators sat with them. One could say what was on one's mind, or not. One could listen to someone else's voiced thoughts, or, hear the voice in one's own head. No one forced his or her beliefs on anyone else. Here, in this place, during meeting for worship, away from the rest of the world, everyone was equal, based on the Quaker belief that there was that of God in everyone. Each person's thoughts were as good as anyone else's. Each person's privacy was as secure as another's. This respect provided a sense of harmony, and peace.

But, Hunter's inner harmony was disturbed by a loud voice to his left, and Hunter remembered that he was not at a meeting for worship. He was at a meeting that addressed problems. And problems brought anything but the feeling of peace.

"I know the intent of this function," said Mark Henry, with patient impatience. "I realize the Faculty Ball is a tradition to show appreciation to the teachers by the Parent Association. But, it is an outmoded tradition. It was originally done when people had little money, and, events, such as this one, were not so expensive. Now, the over-whelming number of families who send their children here are well-to-do, since they are the only ones who can afford the high-priced tuition. The two hundred dollar per person charge for this affair could be put to better use than spending it on an extravagant party. I'm sure most of the underpaid teachers here could use the extra money in their paychecks. I know I could."

He paused. Dr. Falls knew what was coming next. He listened respectfully.

"Dr. Falls," continued Henry, "it could be used to enhance the fund to recruit and pay the tuition for the education of disadvantaged children."

Hunter knew Henry had an ax to grind, but he also had a point. Henry, who was an African-American, could not attend Eastern Friends School when he had applied as a high school student, because his family could not afford the cost. Things had come a long way since then. The school actively recruited talented minority students and offered financial aid. But, there was still this rich men's club atmosphere about the school, which had only been coeducational for a decade. The Faculty Ball was part of that past.

Hunter could see Falls quickly plotting out his diplomatic strategy. Hunter knew the headmaster could not say that events such as the Ball were public relations stunts to cultivate the rich patronage of the school's alumni. From Fall's point of view, it had to do with politics; the ends, and the means to those ends, were often strange bedfellows.

"Mr. Henry," soothed Falls, "you know the Quaker commitment to help others. If God is in everyone, then everyone is worth helping. That is why our students are encouraged to participate in community service. We send volunteer help to nursing homes, the meals-on-wheels program, and shelters for the homeless. We have many drives and fund-raisers during the school year to raise money for charities. And, our more fortunate alumni and parents of current students do their part to help."

"I'm sure," argued Henry, "that we could do much more."

There was a pause.

"I'm sure we could," said Falls, "and we will. But right now I must introduce to all of you Lt. Frank DiSalvo, who is a detective with the Philadelphia Police Department's Homicide Division. He would like to make a brief statement concerning the shocking loss of our alumnus, George Wheeler. I urge you to help him in his investigation."

Hunter had already noticed the man in the well-worn Navy blue suit at the back of the meetinghouse. He had entered quietly at the beginning of the exchange between Dr. Falls and Henry. As he now walked to the center of the meetinghouse, he looked warm, with beads of perspiration on his forehead glistening in the light. But, he did not wipe off the sweat. He did not look uncomfortable. He looked like a man used to the heat. He was medium in height. Hunter noticed, however, that the lieutenant's physical strength could be seen in the policeman's broad shoulders and thick neck. He looked powerfully compact. His hair was dark and curly. He appeared to be a couple of years older than Hunter, who had just turned fifty-five. The lieutenant suddenly flashed a big grin, which softened his hard facial features.

"I'm terribly sorry to disturb your meeting," he said, looking down at the floor, as if he were too out of place to look at those present straight ahead. "I know it is disturbing to talk about a death which involves…foul play."

He then raised his head and looked directly at the audience.

"But, I need your help," he said. "Mr. Wheeler felt very attached to this school. He was an alumnus, and so is his son. He was very instrumental in raising funds for the school. If you can tell me anything about his death, please contact me. Dr. Falls has my telephone number."

He started to leave, but then turned toward the gathering.

"You will be seeing me around the school and its grounds," he said, "and there will be other policemen, also. Please advise your students that it's nothing to be alarmed about."

He flashed the smile again, and continued.

"Just routine procedure. Thank you all very much for your time, and assistance."

Dr. Falls rose from his chair and spoke.

"Thank you, Lieutenant," he said. "The meeting is adjourned. Have a nice evening, everyone."

Hunter turned to Patricia.

"I'll be with you in a minute," he said. "I want to talk to the fuzz."

"OK," said Patricia, "but don't get yourself arrested."

Both Hunter and Mark Henry approached Dr. Falls and the lieutenant, but Henry started talking first.

"Dr. Falls, you know we have to do more concerning the student recruitment program. I think the diverting of the money used for the Faculty Ball to the program would be a sound financial and symbolic act. There are still not enough minority students at this school, not by a long shot."

"I don't think you're giving the school the proper credit it deserves concerning its commitment to the recruitment program, Mr. Henry," said Dr. Falls calmly. "But I promise to meet with you privately to discuss various options. Right now, I think Mr. Hunter has something he would like to say."

Falls looked at Hunter. The Headmaster's eyes revealed a hope that the English teacher would rescue him from a confrontation.

"OK," said Henry, and he added with emphasis, "you state the time. I'll be there, with plenty of suggestions."

He turned abruptly, and walked quickly away.

"Looks like you got yourself a hothead there, Dr. Falls," said Lt. DiSalvo.

Hunter eyed DiSalvo suspiciously. Some old, bad feelings stirred up inside the English teacher about cops.

"Mark Henry is a good teacher, Lieutenant," said Hunter. "And, I think he made some valid points. Just because a person is a member of a minority group and shows some passion when it comes to helping that group, should not make him suspect."

Hunter used the last word purposefully. DiSalvo was silent, looking at Hunter, sizing him up. Dr. Falls looked like he had gone from the frying pan into the fire.

"Now, now, Mr. Hunter," said Falls, trying to change the tone of the conversation. "I'm sure the lieutenant was just making small talk. You came up here to say something to the lieutenant, yes?"

Hunter looked at Falls, then at DiSalvo. He took a breath of air, exhaled, and looked at the ground.

"Yes," he said. "I just wanted to say that I'd like to help with the investigation in any way that I can. I've been trying to refresh my memory since I heard the bad news, but I haven't had time to do any personal research, as of yet. I met Wheeler on a few occasions, and I taught his son, Ronald, in his senior year. I believe it was about ten years ago."

"Did you know anyone who might want George Wheeler harmed, Mr. Hunter?" asked DiSalvo.

"No, not really," answered Hunter. "I know he was involved in some controversies over the initiation of some prescription drugs for use by the public. But, that's common knowledge. I read about it in the newspapers."

"What about Wheeler's son?" asked DiSalvo. "Any thoughts or impressions about him?"

Hunter hesitated, trying to recall what he knew about Ronald Wheeler, and hypothesizing as to DiSalvo's line of questioning.

"Ronald was an OK student. He could have done better. He was always politicking, instead of studying for a higher grade. I believe he was interested in science, joining his father's company, and eventually making a lot of money."

"Thank you for your honest thoughts, Mr. Hunter," said DiSalvo, "and, I appreciate your offer of help."

Before DiSalvo could break away, Hunter had something to say.

"I have a question for you, Lieutenant, if you don't mind."

"Not at all," responded DiSalvo, again showing that disarming smile.

"Wheeler died only two days ago. He was a man about fifty-five, fifty-six years of age?"

"Fifty-six," confirmed DiSalvo.

"At any rate," said Hunter, "he had graduated from here many years ago. Granted, he retained a great deal of interest in the school, but it was hardly the center of his life. He had many contacts, acquaintances, friends, possibly enemies. I'm assuming, given your rank, that you are in charge of the investigation, yes?"

"That is correct, Mr. Hunter." DiSalvo smiled.

"Then why are you here so early in the course of the investigation? I heard on the radio that there were some unusual circumstances surrounding the scene of the crime, but nothing specific was provided. Can you shed some light on this?"

DiSalvo hesitated. Then he spoke.

"We do not divulge certain details in a crime of this nature, because it tends to draw out the compulsive confessors. We can weed out the false confessions by asking questions only the real murderer could answer."

"That's understandable," said Hunter, "but, I

think you can answer my question, and still withhold enough facts to protect the investigation. From what I've read and heard, this killing was thought out. And, your appearance here solidifies a connection with the school. In order for us to help you, you will have to trust us, at least a little."

DiSalvo pondered what Hunter said briefly.

"In Wheeler's lap," said the lieutenant, "we found an Eastern Friends School yearbook. It was issued the year in which Wheeler graduated from this school. The book was open to the page with Wheeler's senior-year picture on it. Someone had drawn a dollar sign over the picture with a green felt pen."

Hunter could feel a slight shiver between his shoulder blades, as if someone close by, unseen, had touched him there with a cold finger. He heard Dr. Falls take a hiss of breath before speaking.

"Of course, we'll do whatever we can to help," he said quietly. Then, trying to lighten the mood slightly, if for no one else except himself, he said, "I know Hunter will want to be involved. He reads all those Ellery Queen and Agatha Christie novels. He loves a mystery."

DiSalvo looked hard and straight at Hunter, aiming his eyes at the teacher's. Then he moved his stare away, as if firing a warning shot.

"This," he said, "is a real one."

FOUR

NOT JUST ANYBODY worked out at the Eastern Men's Athletic Club. Situated near the upscale, downtown Rittenhouse Square area of the city, its members were well-known doctors, lawyers, city officials, and successful businessmen. A large number of the members were alumni of Eastern Friends School, from which the club acquired its name. Thomas Greenstreet Ford, an alumnus of EFS, established it shortly before World War I. Ford had been an Olympic boxer, a winner of the Silver Medal in the middleweight division, and had become one of the city's most famous architects. In the club's early years, a graduate who had participated in varsity sports at EFS was automatically entitled to free EMAC membership at graduation. But, since the students attending EFS had increasingly come from well-to-do families, and the other members of the club were wealthy, and had to be to afford the exorbitant annual fee, the EFS alumni also tended to voluntarily pay the fee.

The money was used to maintain the state-of-the-art athletic equipment, which included saunas, Jacuzzis, an indoor swimming pool, track and squash courts. Subsequently, a bar, a gourmet restaurant, and apartment accommodations for members and guests were added. In recent years, if anyone had accepted the free EFS alumnus membership, that person would have stood out like an old, banged up, used Chevrolet in a parking lot full of shiny new Cadillacs. But that did not stop Robert Fisher.

On this Friday following George Wheeler's death, the day before his funeral, Fisher was at the EMAC, late in the afternoon, as he was every Friday, working out for free. To the small group of young men at the far corner of the gymnasium, who were either working out or toweling off, it always looked as if Fisher was showing off. Whether doing mat routines, or flips on the parallel bars, Fisher appeared to his ex-classmates to be saying, with body language,

"You may have more money than I do. But, I'm better than you at everything else."

It had to be the reason, thought these men, who had graduated with Fisher. He obviously was not there for the company. They knew that he never liked his former schoolmates. He begrudged them their inherited station in life. Fisher had to work after school at the family grocery store, helping his relatives make ends meet. The others felt that the only reason that he accepted the free membership was to defiantly remind them that despite his economic disadvantages, he could always top them. He used to do it at EFS, and not only in athletics. He was a straight "A" student, starred in the school plays, then went on to the University of Pennsylvania on a full scholarship, and graduated from medical school with top honors. But, instead of going into a lucrative practice, Fisher decided to do research in immunology.

As they watched Fisher prepare to work on the horse, they did not notice that Fisher opened and closed his right hand, making a fist, and then releasing the clenched fingers, a number of times. As Fisher mounted and started his routine, it was easy to see why Fisher was nicknamed "Reds."

With his red hair and freckles, he looked like a crimson blur, scissoring and rotating his legs, moving up and down the horse, switching from one hand to the other. Finally, he flung out his legs, flipped them over his head, and finished with a perfect dismount. He grabbed his towel and walked past the observing group of young men.

"Hi, guys," he said with a smirk, and headed for the showers.

"Some nerve," said George Carlisle.

"You would think," said Daniel Lane, "that he would have the decency to express his sympathy to Ronald, here."

They all looked at Ronald Wheeler, who was sitting on an exercise bench.

"Well," he said, "I didn't say anything to him when his mother was killed."

Pierce Bergman raised a blonde eyebrow.

"Feeling a little guilty, Ron?" he asked.

Wheeler gazed up at Bergman's stare.

"Hell, no, Doc," he said. "Just stating a fact. I don't have time for his sympathy, or any self-pity. I now have a business to run. Which reminds me, I want to show all of you a most excellent new toy I have acquired."

Bergman smiled as Wheeler went toward the wall and pulled out what appeared to be a small, slim case from his athletic bag.

"Jason Barnum obtained this for my father from the competition. It was to be used mainly for cataloging drugs and cross-matching that information with files dealing with symptoms of diseases and ailments."

He flipped open the top to reveal a very compact laptop computer.

"It has mucho megabytes. It's great for collating info. It also has a detachable camera cell phone, internal fax/modem, CD-DVD player with burners, and micro web-cam. It's all voice activated. There's wireless internet access, of course. And there's some kind of new battery so I don't have to plug this baby in for a month after it's charged. I have to get in touch with the caterer. With the wake and reception taking place at the house, there are a lot of details to take care of. You're all coming, right?"

"You bet," said Oliver Ford, great grandson of the founder of the EMAC. The others all nodded their heads, except for Daniel Lane.

"I may be tied up a little," he said. "I have to go

to Friends' Hospital in Northeast Philadelphia. My sister has been a patient for about a month, now. I didn't want to say anything. I have to go with my mom. It looks like she will be declared incompetent."

"I'm sorry to hear that," said Bergman. "I have connections at the hospital. If there is anything I can do, let me know."

"Thanks, Pierce," said Lane.

"Well, if you need any help, Ron," said Oliver Ford, "we're there for you. We know it's tough running a business."

"Thanks," said Wheeler, "but I've been involved in the business already. I knew I would have to be ready to step in when Mom died a while back."

Wheeler spoke some commands into the microphone.

"I've got my whole schedule for the next month programmed in, including a meeting with the Board of Directors."

"Speaking of scheduling," said Bergman, "George, my father has a very important patient who wants to sue this company for injuries sustained in a car accident which occurred when he was being chauffeured around in the company limo. I thought your mother would like to know."

Carlisle nodded. His mother, who was an extremely successful lawyer, was helped many times by Bergman's father, Dr. Thomas Bergman, the famous surgeon and hospital director, with these types of referrals.

"I'll set up a meeting," said Carlisle.

"Oliver," said Bergman, "my dad's patient is from out-of-town. Can you set up a stay in one of the luxury suites here?"

"Absolutely no problem." Ford smiled.

"Excellent," said Bergman.

"By the way, Pierce," said Wheeler, "I'd like to meet with your father about marketing that arrhythmia control drug. I knew he and my father were not seeing eye-to-eye over it. But, I think I could smooth things out. Mucho pesos involved, you know."

Bergman's eyes sparkled like icicles in sunlight.

"I'm sure my father will be pleased to hear that," he said. "By the way, you know you shouldn't leave such precious little toys, like your laptop there, just hanging around. There are always certain types trying to get their greedy little hands on things like that."

"Yeah," said Carlisle, "I really had a scare a couple of months ago when I thought someone stole the key to my Porsche. I was really relieved when I found it near my locker compartment, under a bench, a few days later. Boy, was I sick for those few days. I was lost."

"I bet Daniel won't leave that new ring his mother bought him hanging around just anywhere," said Oliver Ford. "Let's have a good look at that Gibraltar look-alike, Dan."

Ford grabbed the left hand of the obviously reluctant Lane, and held up the finger with the huge ruby and gold ring on it.

"Cut it out, Ollie," said the embarrassed Lane. Ford and the others laughed.

"Pierce really did a fine job with the setting, didn't he?" said Ford.

"Anyway," said Pierce, "I want you all to come to my place at the shore after the funeral to, ah, unwind."

"Oh, that sounds like fun," kidded Carlisle. "Are you going to show us more specimens that you have been collecting, Pierce? You must have one of the weirdest collections of dead bugs and animals outside of a natural science museum than anyone in the world. Do you get a discount on formaldehyde?"

"I'm a doctor and a scientist. I take my work home with me. So, sue me," said Bergman.

"I don't know, Pierce," said Carlisle, "I always thought you liked dissecting frogs too much in biology class."

"Well," retaliated Bergman, "after I become as famous a surgeon as my father, you will see how my interests will have paid off."

As they gathered up their equipment, Wheeler decided to rib Bergman, also.

"Pierce," he said, "you never use a towel at this place. Don't you ever sweat?"

Bergman gave him a frosty stare.

"I try not to," he said.

FIVE

As Maxwell Hunter stood in line with Patricia Delvecchio on Saturday morning at the viewing before the funeral, he looked around the Wheeler mansion. It was immense. The room in which they stood was an oval addition to the house, with high, vaulted ceilings and French windows all around. The floor was marble, with a raised platform in the center of the room, which was often used as a stage for private music recitals. George Wheeler had been a patron of the arts, contributing to the Pennsylvania Ballet Company, the Philadelphia Orchestra, the city's Museum of Art, local galleries and individual artists. Many times, in the past, promising performers had been presented for the first time on this platform, on which was now placed the coffin of George Wheeler.

It was a beautiful, though warm, May day. Hunter looked through one group of windows and watched the caterer with his many helpers set up the after-funeral reception on the expansive green lawn. Hunter glanced around and saw that many of his ex-students and their parents had arrived. He also saw some of the current EFS faculty members, including, surprisingly, Mark Henry.

After viewing the body of Wheeler, Hunter and Patricia went to Henry.

"I didn't expect you to be here, Mark," said Hunter. "You didn't know the family, did you?"

Henry stifled a guffaw.

"Oh, yeah, they used to invite me over here all the time," he said sarcastically.

Henry looked around the room.

"Do you see many black people around here, Hunter?" he said. "I mean, outside of the help. Things haven't really changed that much since your beloved sixties, now have they? I figured these high-powered types should see someone different than themselves, who doesn't just clean up. Also, I thought I might lobby a little about the Faculty Ball, among other things."

"I admire your dedication to the cause," said Hunter.

"I don't need your admiration," shot back Henry. "What I need is your help."

"You got it," said Hunter without hesitation.

"Me, too," seconded Patricia.

"Good. Now, if you'll excuse me," he said, and he went off to mingle.

Hunter saw some of his ex-students standing around Ronald Wheeler. He maneuvered Patricia in front of him through the crowd of people, and was hit in the chest by the short-strapped handbag hanging from Patricia's right shoulder as she tried to avoid bumping into someone. As he approached the small group, he shook hands with Ronald.

"I'm sorry I had to see you guys again under these circumstances," he said.

The others made sounds of agreement.

"I know, Ron," continued Hunter, "that it must be tough on you now, since you don't have any brothers or sisters to help you through this difficult time."

"He'll get by, won't you, Ron?" said Pierce Bergman evenly.

"Yeah," said Wheeler, "I can handle the business."

"Well," said Hunter, "I didn't just mean the business."

"I have friends," said Wheeler, "and, taking over the business was what I've been preparing to do for a long time. I'll be just fine."

The others smiled reassuringly.

"Well," said Bergman, "I'm going to find my father. We thought I should be prepared to offer some medical assistance. You know, Valium and such, in case any of the relatives became overwhelmed by the events that have transpired."

He turned to his friends, and said, "Later," and went off carrying a large doctor's bag.

After asking the others how they were doing, Hunter and Patricia excused themselves to help Mark Henry with his mission. Shortly thereafter, Hunter turned to Patricia.

"Let's go," he said, "I've had enough."

"What's the matter?" said Patricia in a needling way. "Feeling a little squeamish?" She knew he hated funerals.

"As you know, not my thing," he said. Hunter had not known death in any close relationship. His parents were still alive and fairly healthy. A few aunts and uncles had died in recent years, and he had managed to avoid the final services. It was his grandmother's funeral, which took place when he was fourteen that he remembered to this day. He could still smell the funeral parlor, with the sickly sweet odor coming from the flowers draped around the casket. The memory had kept him away from similar ceremonies.

"You know," said Patricia, "it is part of reality."

"I'm beginning to confront that more and more as I get older," said Hunter, sadly.

They walked to the car. Hunter opened the door for Patricia. She slid her handbag off of her left shoulder, sat in the seat, and swung her legs inside the car. Hunter closed the door, and went in on the driver's side of the Volkswagen. He tried the engine and it would not turn over. He tried again, without success.

"Damn!" he said, "The mechanic said he fixed the carburetor. He didn't fix anything. These guys are all alike. They take your money and lie to you."

After the fifth try, the car started.

"By the way," said Hunter with a smile," you switched the handbag from the right shoulder to the left."

Patricia smiled back.

"You're good," she said, referring to the little game they often played. "But, I'll catch you yet."

Hunter smiled again.

"Don't bet on it," he said.

SIX

Lt. Frank DiSalvo did not like working on Sundays. It was the one day he tried to forget that he was a policeman. It was the one day he forgot about the murders, the robberies, the drug busts, the homeless, and the con artists. He had even reached the point where he could forget about the time he spent as an Army infantryman in Vietnam. On Sundays, he would sleep until late in the morning in his row house in South Philadelphia, have a nice, relaxing breakfast, and read some Hollywood entertainment magazines or a book he had checked out of the library. He did not read the newspaper, not on Sunday.

He would go to his parents' house in the afternoon for a good old-fashioned Italian meal. Sometimes, he would talk to some friends from the neighborhood. He would often rent an old movie, usually a comedy. He loved the Marx

Brothers. Sometimes, he would go out on a date, as long as the woman knew there was no long-term commitment in the picture. DiSalvo had been married once, and he did not particularly feel like putting a woman he loved through the hell of being a cop's wife, not again.

But on this Sunday, the day after George Wheeler's funeral, DiSalvo was working. Certain crimes, with certain victims, attracted attention. And the quicker they were solved, the happier the public was. And if the public was happy, then DiSalvo's bosses were happy. And that made DiSalvo, if not happy, at least relieved. Besides, this case spooked him a little.

He had spoken with George Wheeler's public relations man, Jason Barnum, earlier in the morning. The information the lieutenant had obtained from him, along with the results of the autopsy, had brought DiSalvo to the home of the eminent Dr. Thomas Bergman.

As DiSalvo drove his four-year-old Ford Taurus into the lengthy driveway leading to the Bergman's Chestnut Hill home, he made out the form of a woman coming out of a rear door of the house. A man followed her as she approached the

Jaguar parked in front of the three-car garage. As DiSalvo pulled up, he heard the woman call out.

"If you think, Thomas," said the woman, "that I am going to hang around this boring house all Sunday, you're crazy! I'm going shopping, and afterward, I'll do whatever else suits me."

She was blonde, in her upper forty's, quite beautiful, with long, lovely legs, which she did not mind showing off by wearing a short tight skirt. She hopped into the car, gunned the engine, and threw it into first gear, causing the wheels to spin savagely, bringing the smell of burnt rubber to DiSalvo's nose. The Jaguar veered almost out of control temporarily, and the front bumper knocked over some large potted plants on the edge of the driveway, before it righted itself in an arc-like motion, and then sped down the driveway.

DiSalvo got out of his car and approached the man standing in front of the garage.

"Dr. Thomas Bergman, I presume," he said, holding up his badge. "I'm Lieutenant Frank DiSalvo of the Philadelphia Police Department. I'm investigating the death of George Wheeler. Sorry to barge in on you, but I must ask you a few questions."

DiSalvo's approach was mannerly, but firm. He did not want to give the doctor the chance to put him off to a later time.

"Well, nice to meet you, Lieutenant," said Bergman. "I'm sorry you had to witness one of my wife's little tantrums."

DiSalvo flashed one of his disarming smiles.

"That's quite alright," he said, "although, I would have liked to have spoken to her—Kelly, I believe is your wife's first name, is that right?"

"Correct," responded Dr. Bergman. "Let's go inside, Lieutenant."

He turned to a couple of housekeepers who were doing lawn work, and asked them to clean up the knocked-over plants. DiSalvo noticed that the two women were already in the process of moving toward the debris, looking as if they were used to cleaning up after the boss's wife.

Dr. Bergman guided DiSalvo into a huge glass-enclosed patio, which housed an indoor pool and bar, along with a lounge area. DiSalvo sat down on one of the floral-designed cushioned chairs.

"Can I get you something, Lieutenant?" asked the doctor.

"A ginger ale would be nice," said DiSalvo.

Bergman looked up at the warm light shining in through the glass.

"The sun can make it uncomfortable in here sometimes," he said. "Let's see if we can make it a little cooler."

"I'm fine," said DiSalvo.

Bergman ignored the remark and from behind the bar, he pushed some buttons. Air conditioning fans started to whir at high speed. Motorized shades, bunched together at the peak of the curved ceiling, were drawn downwards on tracks that ribbed the walls, providing substantial shade. Dr. Bergman handed DiSalvo his drink.

"I'll get right to the point," said the lieutenant. "The autopsy report shows that George Wheeler was knocked out with a blunt instrument, possibly the handle of a gun, and was injected with an overdose of digitalis, causing a complete heart block. I spoke with Jason Barnum, who told me Wheeler's company was almost ready to request FDA approval of a new arrhythmia control drug, but that Wheeler wanted more time to evaluate its potential for allergic reactions, since it tested positive in this regard with a rather significant percentage of control group users. Barnum said you were pressuring Wheeler to quit delaying submission, because of promises made by you concerning expedited use of the drug by a large network of medical acquaintances. Barnum suggested you had a great deal to gain monetarily by this transaction. The word "kickback" was used. He also noted that you had pressured Wheeler on premature usage of other drugs, in one case practically endorsing a placebo for migraine headache sufferers, and once causing a number of lawsuits to come to pass concerning a diabetes control medication. He implied that you used considerable influence in lobbying for approval by the FDA on drugs in the past."

DiSalvo stopped, sipped his drink, and waited to see how Bergman would respond to this assault. The doctor handled it quite coolly.

"You are obviously an intelligent man," said Bergman, "and one who does his research. That research has, I am sure, informed you of my, if I may be so bold, respected reputation in the medical profession. Through my leadership, many breakthroughs have been expedited in the field of medicine, and many people have been helped in time to save them from pain, suffering, and even death. Sometimes there have been, how should I put it, poor judgment calls, and a few have suffered. But, all in all, the overwhelming majority have benefited from my medical decisions. I did consultation work for Mr. Wheeler; nothing underhanded was involved. But, his reluctance to move quickly in the use of certain drugs on occasion was not due to any humanitarian reasons. He was a small-minded man, looking only at how transactions affected him, how he would look if something went wrong, how he would fare monetarily if lawsuits were brought to bear. In any event, Wheeler and I agreed much more often than we disagreed on these matters. So let's not blow this point out of proportion. Can I get you a refill?"

"Yes, thank you," said DiSalvo coolly. He accepted the drink, stared into the ice in the glass, and then looked back at Bergman. He pressed on.

"Dr. Bergman," he said, "Mr. Barnum had more to say. You have to understand that I must ask questions even though they may make you uncomfortable, because of the severity of the crime committed." He paused. "Mr. Barnum noted several visits by your wife to Mr. Wheeler's office. He stated that he observed them together on numerous occasions, when Barnum would drop Wheeler off at a location downtown. The possibility of a liaison was raised. Did you know of anything that was going on between Wheeler and your wife?"

Dr. Bergman fixed DiSalvo with a glacial stare.

"First," he said, "Jason Barnum is a reptile, Lieutenant. You have been listening to a man who works in advertising; he lies for a living. To my knowledge, there is no truth to his accusation. It sounds to me as if the man is trying to throw suspicion off of himself onto someone else. After all, he was the one at the scene of the crime. Now, I'll tell you something you possibly did not hear from Barnum. Wheeler was ready to dump him. He felt Barnum's advertising campaigns were promising too much. As I said before, Wheeler mostly thought only about his own skin, and did not want to get into any trouble with the public. Now, is there anything else, Lieutenant?"

Lt. DiSalvo was not the only one seeing and hearing Dr. Thomas Bergman. In a room upstairs, that was filled with television screens monitoring the security of the home, Pierce Bergman and his younger brother, Mansfield, listened to the conversation between the policeman and their father.

"Dad is quite good, isn't he?" said Mansfield, lying on a leather couch, looking at a Playboy Magazine.

"Yes, Manny, that he is," said Pierce, as he manipulated a console which controlled various camera angles and zoom lenses. He turned to his brother.

"Manny," he said, "Do you love Mom and Dad?"

Manny flipped through the pages of the magazine, lingering over a certain preferred photograph.

"Absolutely," he said. "I love that we lucked out and have such wealthy parents. How else would we have been able to get all this good stuff?"

He stopped. Then he continued.

"But, Dad kind of goes overboard with some of that charity stuff. You know, giving away things, money, doing hospital fund-raising drives. It seems to me that you shouldn't have to feel guilty about having money. That's what this country is about."

Pierce smiled.

"Oh, it's not guilt," he said. "It's just all part of the game. You see, if you want to stay rich, and get richer, you have to show that rich is good, that rich people are noble, and generous, and that everyone benefits from that wealth. So, you throw a few thousand dollars here and there, making sure it is tax-deductible, of course."

Manny laughed, and flipped pages.

Well," he said, "after I graduate from EFS this year, I'm going to college, and then med school to specialize in cosmetic surgery. And, I'm going to use Dad's name and connections to add to the family wealth, by making people happy. Because, as Billy Crystal's Fernando used to say, 'You know, darling, looking good is better than feeling good.'"

They both laughed. Pierce looked at a TV screen.

"I do believe that the lieutenant has almost finished," he said.

Lt. DiSalvo was heading for the door.

"Dr. Bergman," he said, "doesn't it seem strange that George Wheeler was in the process of marketing an arrhythmia control drug and was killed with an overdose of a heart medication? Do you have any thoughts on that?"

"It's interesting," responded the elder Bergman, "but, other than that, I have no other comments on the matter."

His tone sounded final.

"Dr. Bergman," said DiSalvo, "I must ask you this question before I leave. For the record, where were you last Monday morning, between 6:30 and 7:30 a.m.?"

"I was driving to the hospital," answered the doctor, "as I usually do on Mondays. I am used to starting the workweek early. Patients do not stop getting sick for their doctor's convenience. A physician's work is never done."

"And you were alone?" asked DiSalvo.

"Of course," said Bergman, as if any other answer would have been absurd.

"Very well, Doctor," said DiSalvo. "Thank you for your time. But, I will have to question Mrs. Bergman. I can either do it here, or, if she prefers, downtown."

He shot a hard look at Bergman.

"I understand, Lieutenant," said Bergman, "I'll tell her when she returns."

"I'm sure you will, sir," he said, and abruptly turned to leave. He had developed a great desire to get away. He was suddenly angry that his Sunday had been taken away from him.

SEVEN

IT WAS A SUNNY SATURDAY, one week after the funeral of George Wheeler. Joseph Wilson would like to have been in his own back yard, working on his old Ford Mustang. But, it was his turn to work the weekend shift at the sprawling suburban estate of Elizabeth Carlisle in West Chester, Pennsylvania, just outside of Philadelphia. "Handyman" was a good description for Wilson, since he was quite adept at working with his hands. Today, he was fine-tuning Ms. Carlisle's Cadillac limousine. (She had always said to him, "Call me Betsy," but Wilson never felt comfortable using such a familiar nickname. So he always used her last name.)

As he worked on the Caddy, he thought that there would never be a foreign-made car on this property, not with Ms. Carlisle's daddy being a major stockholder of General Motors. Not that she didn't earn enough money herself to buy any car she wanted. She had used her head start in life to become one of the most successful attorneys in the East.

Wilson did like being on the Carlisle homestead, though, even if it was a weekend. It reminded him of the wide-open country of the Mid-West, where he grew up on his parents' farm. He had come east to make a living, but he always thought about returning to the farm when he stared out over the Carlisle grounds.

It was while these thoughts filled his mind, that he saw the horse. It was one of Ms. Carlisle's thoroughbreds. She rode her horses around the property every weekend. She had done so this Saturday morning. But, the horse he now saw had no rider.

Wilson ran to the horse as it came close to the garage. It was used to him. He grabbed the reins, patted the side of its nose, and led the horse to the stables. After he had returned the horse to its stall, he ran to the kitchen and told one of the maids on duty what had happened. Since the property was so large, each took one half of the property to search for Ms. Carlisle.

Wilson drove for about an hour, and finally headed for the dirt road that skirted the property near the brook on the far eastern side. He stopped the car, and walked among the trees, since the pick-up could not travel in the densely forested area. He had done this at various spots around the property, without success. While he looked, he decided the horse must have become frightened, and thrown its rider. He continued to scan the area. He saw something red near a distant tree. He jogged in that direction, and slowly made out a woman's form. As he approached, he realized it was Ms. Carlisle, wearing her red and black riding costume, lying in a shallow ditch in the ground. He started to refresh his memory rapidly about CPR, thought about calling an ambulance on the cellular phone, but, the closer he got, the more worried he became. She was motionless; there appeared to be no breathing. He knelt down beside her to feel her pulse. Nothing. A thin, but deep cut had been made on her throat, and the blood oozing from the wound was soaking the riding jacket with its matching color. Blood also dripped from her mouth, leaving stains on both sides of her lips. Wilson noticed that what was apparently Ms. Carlisle's wristwatch had been removed and placed across her chest. Its face had been smashed.

Wilson felt a surge of nausea, which was suddenly held in check by curiosity. Amid the redness, he saw a glint of silver. He looked closer at Ms. Carlisle's mouth. As he peered at her open lips, he saw that between her teeth, almost ready to fall out, was a shiny coin.

EIGHT

MAXWELL HUNTER TOOK the bucket full of water that was situated under the leak in Patricia Delvecchio's kitchen, and replaced it with an empty one. He emptied the full bucket into the kitchen sink, and then placed it on the floor, ready to be reused. He had just arrived at Patricia's townhouse for dinner on this rainy Sunday, the day after Betsy Carlisle's body had been found.

Patricia's house was located in the Philadelphia neighborhood of Roxborough, which was only about a five-minute drive from Eastern Friends School. The area was made up of white-collar and blue-collar workers, professionals, and self-employed business people. The section was primarily Irish-Catholic, but its closeness to the center of the city brought a variety of people from different backgrounds to live there, especially in apartment houses. For this reason, the hilly area was often referred to as the "Ethnic Alps." Patricia liked the area, particularly for its down-to-earth people, and its closeness both to work and the cultural center of the city.

"Did you call the District Attorney's office about the roof scam?" he asked Patricia.

"Yes, I did," answered Patricia. "They said there are hundreds of people who have filed claims who are expected to be compensated. But, it will take time."

Hunter shook his head.

"It still gets me. These people went under the names of various roofing companies, told people they would charge a small amount to do minor repairs, opened up the roofs, making their victims vulnerable, told the customers that things were much worse, and then raised the prices astronomically. Many times they didn't fix a thing, as in your case."

Patricia watched Hunter fume. She was much more philosophical about these things, putting them into a bigger perspective, and did not get so upset, as did Max. Not that she wasn't appropriately outraged.

"You know, this was done on such a large

scale," she said as she picked up the teapot from the back burner of the stove to pour Hunter a cup of hot coffee, and returned the kettle to where it had been. "That's very American. Brash. Dishonesty in a big way. In Europe, I remember many petty con artists. But, the only place you would find such notorious corruption was usually in the governments, where it was expected."

As she turned to finish preparing the salad she had taken out of the refrigerator, Patricia bumped into the side of the teakettle at the front of the stove.

"You moved it," said Hunter as he sipped his coffee.

"What?" asked Patricia, trying to hide a sly smile.

"You wanted to see if I would notice that you moved the kettle onto the front burner," said Hunter. "You did it when your body blocked the stove as you were going for the salad in the refrigerator."

She laughed.

"You are good," she admitted.

Hunter leaned back in his chair, folded his hands behind his neck, and smiled at her.

"Have you thought about taking that trip to France and Italy this summer?" she asked. "There's still time to book a flight for us you know."

"I'm not sure," said Hunter, looking away from Patricia. "I have plenty of work to do this summer, preparing new thematic units for the next school year."

Patricia shook her head.

"Don't be so work-ethic American," she said. "I'll take you to the Louvre, and Notre Dame in Paris. We'll have quiche and wine for lunch in the Tuileries, and sit by the Seine at night and watch the *bâteaux mouches* float by. In Italy, we'll have a large meal in the middle of the day with the rest of the Italians, who are smart enough to know that even in the middle of the work day, you should pause for a long, good feast. You don't have to go into the museums to see good art in Italy. It is in the squares in Rome and Florence, where you can admire the architecture and sculpture while you dine."

"OK, OK, you've convinced me," yielded Hunter.

Patricia brought out the veal she had cooked,

still hot in the pan, and placed it on the table with her right hand. She went back to the oven and brought out the piping hot bread, and placed the pan under Hunter's nose with her left hand.

Hunter smelled the food.

"Everything looks delicious," he said, as Patricia sat down at the table, "and I noticed that you switched the oven mitten from your right hand to the left in between taking out the veal and the bread. Salute!" Hunter lifted his wine glass.

"Bravo!" Patricia responded.

"And," he said, "since I cooked last week, and you washed the dishes, I shall return the favor this week."

Soon after they started eating, Patricia looked at Hunter, as he poked at his veal with his fork.

"You're preoccupied," she said. "What's the matter? Is it the Carlisle woman?" They had heard the news on the radio that morning.

"Yes," he said. "Two murders now. And, not only connected to the school, but also to two students I taught. I came to this school to teach because I thought that the Quaker belief that there is that of the divine in everyone naturally implies that it is forbidden to harm another. That's also what I believed when I was a student in college during the Sixties. I worked with Quakers back then, joined them in peace marches and fasts to help fight against violence because we shared a respect for the sanctity of the individual. Now, someone is striking directly at that belief, and I'm frightened."

Patricia reached out across the table, covered Hunter's hand with her own, and squeezed it.

The telephone rang.

"I'll get it," said Hunter.

Hunter walked to the phone that was on a lamp table next to the sofa in the living room. He sat down on the sofa, and picked up the receiver.

"Hello," he said.

"Hello, Hunter? This is Lt. DiSalvo."

Hunter, surprised to hear the policeman's voice, did not respond right away.

"Hunter, are you there?" DiSalvo asked.

"Yes," said Hunter. "How did you know I would be here?"

"I am a detective, you know," chuckled DiSalvo. "When I couldn't reach you at your place, I thought you might be at Miss Delvecchio's home."

"Good work," said Hunter a little coldly, "but then you guys are used to invading other people's privacy.

"I'm sorry," said DiSalvo, "but I'm calling to take you up on your offer of help. You must have heard about the death of Ms. Carlisle."

"Yes," said Hunter. He looked down at the book on the coffee table in front of him. It was Dante's *Divine Comedy*. The book was open, and he saw that Patricia had been reading from *Il Paradiso*.

"I'd be glad to help in any way I can, Lieutenant," said Hunter.

"OK. I'll meet you in an hour at your place," declared DiSalvo.

"My place, in an hour?" Hunter was somewhat taken aback. "Isn't that a little quick? You sure you don't want me to come downtown?"

"Hunter," said DiSalvo, "you've been watching too many cop shows on TV. Anyway, no point in putting it off. See you in an hour."

Patricia walked in from the kitchen a few seconds later.

"Pat…" Hunter started to say.

"I heard. It's OK. I was just putting together a doggy bag for you," she said.

She sat down next to him, and kissed him. She looked at the coffee table, picked up the book, and looked at the passage from *L'Inferno*.

"You opened the book to a different page," she said. "You see, two can play at this game."

And then she hugged him.

NINE

Lt. Frank DiSalvo was waiting for Maxwell Hunter to arrive at the teacher's Montgomery County townhouse just outside the Philadelphia city limits. The rain had let up, which, thought DiSalvo, was the only good news about this second Sunday in a row on which he had to work. He looked around the housing development. It was modern, clean, very suburban, very safe-looking. But then, he thought, Elizabeth Carlisle probably thought that she was safe where she had lived, also.

He had received a call very early that morning from his captain, who had been contacted by the suburban police. After officers had arrived at the Carlisle estate, one of the policemen noticed an EFS class graduation picture at the home. Since information was always shared between the metropolitan police departments, the West Chester office knew about the Wheeler case. DiSalvo had been out early to the Carlisle house, and the morgue where Ms. Carlisle's body had been transferred. After getting the details, DiSalvo knew he was up against a serial killer, a real strange one.

He saw Hunter pull up in his Volkswagen. They exchanged hello's, and Hunter let the lieutenant enter his home. He offered DiSalvo a cup of coffee, which the lieutenant accepted, and they sat down in Hunter's living room.

"Well, Lieutenant," said Hunter, "you said you wanted my help. I thought I might be on your suspect list by now."

DiSalvo sipped his coffee, and used the same smile Hunter had seen at their last encounter.

"Not any more than anyone else associated with the school," he said.

"Yes, but I taught the children of both people who have been murdered," said Hunter.

"OK, if you want to be investigated, where were you when the two murders took place?" asked DiSalvo through his smile.

"On the day of Wheeler's death, I was having breakfast with a student, James Learner, at a

McDonald's just before the school day began. However, I have a feeling you already knew that," said Hunter.

"Yes," said DiSalvo, "I did. And I would guess that Ms. Delvecchio would provide an alibi for yesterday, since you both were supposed to go to a, to a …" (DiSalvo pulled out a notebook) "symposium at Westmont Friends School on 'The role of the Quaker school in an affluent society'."

"You would be correct," said Hunter, a bit sharply. "Is there anything else you want to tell me about myself?"

"Well," said DiSalvo as he flipped a page, "when you were a college student, you participated in a number of demonstrations against the Vietnam War, and for the Civil Rights Movement. It says here that you were a member of the Student Mobilization Committee to End the War in Vietnam. You were arrested a number of times in peaceful sit-ins. Once, in Washington, D. C., things got out of hand at a rally in the summer of 1970, and you were booked for resisting arrest."

"Yeah," said Hunter heatedly, "I banged my head into a cop's nightstick, and forced my face into a spray can of Mace. You guys ought to have some of that stuff tried on you. Then maybe you wouldn't be ready to use it so quickly."

"Cool down, Hunter," said DiSalvo.

"I see the local Gestapo has really been checking up on me," said Hunter, refusing to douse his anger.

"I said I wanted your help, and I meant it," said DiSalvo, "but, I had to check you out."

"Well, you know all about me, but I don't know anything about you, Lieutenant," continued Hunter. "While I was being a menace to America, what were you doing?"

There was a pause. DiSalvo did not like this, but realized they had to get this behind them before they could work together.

"I was an Army infantryman in Vietnam," he finally said.

"Oh, I see," said Hunter, as he gave DiSalvo an exaggerated salute, "So you couldn't stop wearing a weapon. You liked toting a gun so much, you went and became a cop."

"Look," said DiSalvo, who did not nearly show how really pissed off he was, "for your information, I was drafted; I didn't volunteer. And I hated being there. And I didn't like the fact that we got into that war, and I didn't like the way we fought it."

He stopped. He collected his thoughts, and made his pitch.

"Look, I'm not the villain in this story. I'm not locking up any political prisoners. I'm trying to go after the bad guy, or gal, who kills people. The reason I checked you out was because I had to know if I could trust you with details of the case. I was impressed with your deductive reasoning, the way you used the information you already had, to figure out why I had come to EFS. After realizing from your record that helping a cop was the last thing you would want to do, I decided you were sincere in offering me assistance. I can use someone on the inside. People clam up in front of cops. You are a familiar, unthreatening presence, and people will feel more relaxed around you. Others may open up, possibly providing something useful. You also are at the school all the time. I don't have the manpower to cover the situation that completely. Finally, you have the link with the past, since you taught the children of the victims. That's why I'm here, asking for your help."

DiSalvo's speech had the intended effect on Hunter. The teacher calmed down as he listened to the lieutenant. Hunter thought for a while before speaking.

"You said that things have changed," said Hunter, "and that you're not the villain. OK. I guess things have changed. But the story can easily be rewritten. Just change a few events, a character here and there, and, as quick as ink dries on a page, the good guys can look like bad guys, and the other way around. All I know is that if you try to resist the system, the system tries to remove the resistance. And, it brings in the mechanics with the hardware to put in the fix. It just depends on when that resistance takes place, or where. It could be Jesus Christ or Charles Manson."

Hunter stopped. He took a deep breath, and exhaled slowly.

So," he said, "for now we're after a killer, and we both agree we have to get this person. And, Ms. Delvecchio gave me enough food for two. So, let's eat, and talk."

DiSalvo smiled. He was relieved, and hungry.

TEN

As THEY ATE, both men avoided conversation about the crimes, and made small talk about the weather, food, and restaurants. They finished the meal with a cup of coffee and a piece of Patricia's carrot cake, which was covered with cream cheese icing and chocolate shavings. After they had eaten, they both felt relaxed, refreshed, and ready to go to work on their task.

"You have to tell Ms. Delvecchio that she is one hell of a cook," said DiSalvo. "Because I'm Italian she'll appreciate the compliment more."

"I'll tell her," said Hunter. He paused. "Now, what did you come to tell me?"

DiSalvo took a last sip of coffee, and told Hunter the details of how George Wheeler was found. He noticed the look on Hunter's face go from shock, to morbid curiosity, to worry.

"The ashes on the face," interrupted Hunter,

"that's why you were interested in Mark Henry after hearing his speech." There was a tone of apology in his voice.

"I had to consider the racial angle because of the evidence," said DiSalvo, "not because of prejudice. Despite all its good intentions, the school is primarily supported by those who are white and well-to-do. An angry person could see the school as just another way that the white man keeps money and power to himself. Especially someone like Henry, who I found out, tried to gain admittance to EFS when he was young, but could not afford it."

DiSalvo recounted the information concerning the cause of Wheeler's death by injection of an overdose of digitalis, which was administered after he was rendered unconscious. He also told Hunter about the dispute with Dr. Thomas Bergman over the use of the new heart drug, the doctor's lobbying with the FDA, as well as Mrs. Bergman's possible involvement with George Wheeler.

"I talked to Ronald Wheeler," said DiSalvo, "and he was just like you said. He seemed as if he hardly had time on his agenda for mourning. By the way, he said he was on his way to the office at the time of his dad's death. He said he didn't jog with his father because he did his workouts at the, ah, Eastern Men's Athletic Club. I have an appointment tomorrow, 'downtown,' as you said, with Mrs. Bergman. That's where she wanted the interview. When there was just one murder, I thought there was something there. Now, I'm not so sure. I'm also scheduled to talk to George Carlisle."

"Tell me about the Carlisle murder," said Hunter.

DiSalvo told Hunter about how Betsy Carlisle was found in a ditch, her broken watch lying across her chest, her throat slit, and with a coin in her mouth.

"A shiny silver dollar," said DiSalvo.

"That does add emphasis to the rich angle," said Hunter.

"And if that's not weird enough," said DiSalvo, "listen to this. Elizabeth Carlisle had two teeth removed, one from each side of her mouth."

There was a silence, as the strange facts laid out by DiSalvo sat there in front of Hunter for him to mentally grasp, and regard. DiSalvo could see this Sixties suburban boy fighting the instinct to cringe, to retreat from the gruesome reality being thrust at him.

"OK, OK," said Hunter, more to settle himself than for any other reason. "Let's just go over what these two crimes have in common."

"Well," said DiSalvo, "the victims both had boys who graduated approximately nine or ten years ago."

"Right," confirmed Hunter. "Ronald Wheeler was a senior when George Carlisle was a junior. They became acquainted through playing sports and being part of the same social circles."

"So," continued DiSalvo, "the students and parents knew each other. We're not talking strangers, here."

"What about the current family and professional situation involving the two families?" asked Hunter.

"There were no strong social or professional bonds between George Wheeler and Elizabeth Carlisle," said DiSalvo. "The children followed in the parents' footsteps. You know about Ronald. George Carlisle is a junior partner in a prominent law firm, with which his mother had done business."

"I had heard about the death of Ronald's mother a few years back," said Hunter. "I don't recall ever finding out much about George's father."

"You're right about Mrs. Wheeler," said DiSalvo, "and I have to find out more from George about his father. His parents were divorced. Preliminary information is that George's dad split when the boy was quite young."

"So," said Hunter, "both victims were single. And, I believe, both Ronald and George are only children, right?"

"Correct," confirmed the lieutenant.

Hunter paused.

"There are some items of a medical nature that we have to explore," said Hunter. "George Wheeler was involved in pharmacology. He was killed by a drug overdose. Ms. Carlisle had teeth removed."

Hunter was not sure he wanted to hear the answer to his next question.

"How were the teeth, ah, extracted?" he asked.

"It was pretty messy," said DiSalvo, almost

getting a macabre pleasure out of telling Hunter the gory details. "A lot of quick cutting and pulling. The knife used was probably sharp. Could be the same one that cut her throat. Was it a scalpel? Don't know. Early reports indicate that a skilled person did not have to be involved. Hopefully we'll know more from the forensic staff soon."

"Anything else?" asked Hunter.

DiSalvo shook his head.

"I wish there was. Any suggestions?" he asked.

Hunter thought for a few seconds.

"There was a group of my former students who attended EFS at the same time that Ronald and George did," he said. "They used to hang out together back then, and apparently still do, since I saw them at the Wheeler funeral. I can give you their names."

"You don't have to," said DiSalvo. "I had a couple of plain-clothes men at the Wheeler house. With that EFS yearbook in Wheeler's lap, I figured I'd better have some security at a gathering of so many people associated with the school. I'll have a couple of officers at the Carlisle funeral this Saturday, also. I may be there, too."

"Look," said Hunter, "I want permission to

recruit people to help me out: Ms. Delvecchio, and my student, James Learner. Patricia can catch what I may miss among the adults, and James can cover the student body. I trust them."

DiSalvo rubbed his chin. He did not like it, but again was persuaded by Hunter's logic.

"OK, then," said the lieutenant. "Oh, there was one more thing. Something was stolen from Ronald Wheeler on the day of the funeral. It was a high-tech laptop computer he had just acquired. Apparently it was Ronald's favorite current plaything. He seemed to be overly concerned about the loss of it, when I talked to him, considering that he had just lost his father."

Maxwell Hunter leaned back in his chair, and looked at the ceiling.

"Curiouser, and curiouser," he said.

ELEVEN

DR. NICHOLAS SCOTT sat in the hospital cafeteria across from his colleague, Robert "Reds" Fisher, on the Monday after Elizabeth Carlisle's death. Scott was finishing his lunch, and observed the hardly touched meal of his companion. He spoke to the newspaper that was hiding Fisher's face.

"Hey, Reds," he said, "you better get some food under your belt. We have a long afternoon-into-the-evening ahead of us, reviewing the results of those retrovirus studies."

Fisher did not seem to hear him. He had borrowed Scott's paper, saying that he had wanted to read about the murder of Betsy Carlisle. Fisher had hardly said anything during lunch. But Scott now heard him speak softly, but coldly.

"Good. Good," he said. "Let them know what it's like. What it's like to have your parent ripped away from you. They always had everything a buck could buy. Well, let's see how they handle a little family downsizing."

Scott shuddered a little as he heard the menace in Fisher's voice.

"Easy, now, Reds," he said cautiously. "I know you've had a hard history. But, let's listen to what we're saying here, old friend."

Fisher lowered the newspaper. His hardened face slowly softened, and then emitted a laugh.

"Sorry," he said. "I shouldn't let the past get to me so much."

Scott felt himself become physically relieved.

"Let's get back to work, OK?" he said.

"OK," said Fisher.

TWELVE

LT. FRANK DISALVO was catching up on paperwork in his office on that same Monday, as he
waited for Mrs. Kelly Bergman to appear for her
interview. She was already over an hour late. He
was reviewing the information he had on Dr.
Thomas Bergman's wife when Sergeant Edgar
told him that she had arrived. Mrs. Bergman came
into the office looking quite stunning. She was
wearing a dark, short dress. She had on diamond
earrings and a pearl necklace. She sat down
without being invited, put down her bag of bought
things, and crossed her legs. She tossed her
blonde hair back, and flashed a seductive smile,
as disarming as any DiSalvo had in his arsenal.

"Guess I'm a bit tardy," she said. "I just had to
stop at Bloomingdale's. But, I wouldn't have
missed this little chat for the world. I get to see
all of these strong, brave policemen at work. Very

exciting. Actually most of the people I usually meet are, frankly, boring."

DiSalvo returned fire with his grin.

"Even George Wheeler?" he asked.

"Ah, right to the point, I see," said Mrs. Bergman. "No, George was more interesting than most of the already rich snobs I usually run across. His family was well off, and they were able to provide George with a good education. But, later, his parents had trouble with some bad investments. George was forced to earn his own money as an adult, work his way up. It added a certain aggressive excitement to his conversations."

"Just his conversations?" asked DiSalvo.

"Why, Lieutenant, whatever are you implying?" said Mrs. Bergman, but she smiled as she said it, and her tone was one of mock outrage.

"Well, Mrs. Bergman, there are rumors," said DiSalvo, "that you may have been more than just friends with George Wheeler. I must pursue this line of questioning since I must explore possible motives surrounding his unfortunate death." He added intimately, in a low voice, and with a smile, "You understand, don't you?"

"Yes," she responded in kind, "I do. But that's all they were—rumors. Is there anything else you would like to ask me?" she added, as she leaned back and uncrossed and crossed her legs.

"I found out, just in passing," said DiSalvo, "that you were once employed as a nurse. What made you go into that field, and why did you leave?"

"Well," she said, "Daddy was a doctor before he retired, and it seemed a shame to let all those good medical books go to waste. But, I didn't want to become a doctor, not that I wasn't smart enough; what I really wanted was to marry a doctor. The ones hanging around my father were much too old. So, what better place to meet young, good-looking ones than at a top-rated hospital. And that's where I met Thomas."

In the same kind of cutesy, small, intimate voice, DiSalvo said, "There's a little tidbit that I have here that says there was a little problem once while you were on staff at the hospital, something about a patient on one of your rounds getting the wrong medication, and going into anaphylactic shock. I think the word 'negligence' was mentioned. Anything you might want to clear up about this incident?"

"Well, well," she said, "Thomas said you were a good little researcher, and, I see that you are! Well then, you must already know I was cleared of any, ah, wrongdoing."

"Just one more, small thing, then." DiSalvo smiled. "Would you tell me where you were on the morning that George Wheeler was killed?"

"Yes," she said seductively, "I was in bed. Unfortunately alone. That is to say, I have no alibi. Thomas and my son, Pierce, had gone off to work, and my other son, Mansfield, had stayed at a friend's house for the weekend. He had gone straight to school from there. The house staff did not arrive until later."

"And where were you this past Saturday morning," continued DiSalvo, "at the time of Elizabeth Carlisle's death?"

"Oh yes, Betsy Carlisle, what a shame," she said, but there was enough revealed in Kelly Bergman's voice which implied that, as far as Mrs. Bergman was concerned, it was no shame at all.

"Well," she said, holding up her bag from Bloomingdale's, which was so small, DiSalvo guessed it contained jewelry, "I was shopping."

"What was your relationship with Ms. Carlisle?" asked DiSalvo, pursuing a hunch.

"Nothing much," she said. "Thomas referred clients to her, and provided some medical research information for her law practice. Other than that, it was just things having to do with the boys and school. You know, a few committees, social events, and such."

She allowed for a slight pause.

"Well," she said, "unless we get to hold hands while you fingerprint me, I really think I should be going, Lieutenant."

DiSalvo got up and offered his hand.

"Thank you for coming," he said.

Mrs. Bergman stretched out her naked hand, and held DiSalvo's briefly, but tightly.

"My pleasure," she said, and quickly picked up her things and left.

As DiSalvo sat down and gathered his paperwork, he heard a bit of a commotion outside. Sergeant Edgar came into the office, holding a cup in his hand, his shirt wet from a large coffee stain.

"I hope you don't invite her here again," he said gruffly to DiSalvo. "She whipped her bag around and knocked the coffee onto my shirt."

He started to pat the stain with a washroom paper towel.

"She didn't even have the decency to apologize," he growled.

THIRTEEN

MAXWELL HUNTER HAD just finished his last-period class on Wednesday afternoon. As the students rushed through the doorway, James Learner came up to Hunter's desk.

"So, how are things in the independent study world of Gothic fiction?" asked Hunter.

"It's frightfully hard work," joked Learner, "but I'm heavily into Poe and his use of the doppelganger."

"Ah, then you must be beside yourself," smiled Hunter.

"As a matter of fact, I am," said Learner. "On the one hand I am Jimmy Learner, all-around student. I am also your undercover agent, James 'Bond' Learner, and I have dug up some poop on the recent evil goings-on. Should we get out our decoder rings?"

"Just cut to the chase," said Hunter. Sometimes, he thought, James did not know when to quit. But he was grateful that both James and Patricia had agreed to help him.

"Well," said Learner, "I was talking to Mansfield, alias Manny, Bergman today. He's on the debating team with me. I never saw a guy argue both sides of an issue with equal ease the way he does. I finally realized it's because he has no point of view. He just wants to win. And, he often does, impressively. He'll say anything to a girl to get her to go out with him. I have to admire his success with the females. Anyway, since you told me that Lt. DiSalvo was investigating his parents, I thought I'd bring up the murders. I asked him if he thought the police suspected his parents. He said he didn't see why anyone would think that his father would want to hurt anyone who had been so 'nice' to him. I said who would that be. And he said Betsy Carlisle. And I asked what did he mean by 'nice'? He then gave me a wink, and that old male locker room elbow nudge, and walked away with a dirty smile on his face. I think Manny thinks he's a blue chip off of the old block."

Hunter shook his head.

"This is turning into some lousy soap opera," he said. "And, don't be so caught up with Manny's accomplishments. I think he's one of those cheaters I told you about. Do you know anything about his involvement?"

"No," said Learner, as he looked away.

Hunter suspected that he did, but did not press, for now.

"So, have you made any progress?" asked Learner.

"Not really," said Hunter. "I have a few ideas. None of them is very good. I'm trying to get some of the papers and blue books that I put into storage with the school's records department. I only archived stuff from the end of the school year, which was not returned to students. I like to keep this material so I can use it for examples of how students dealt with the material in the past. It's been quite a few years since the boys of the victims went to school here. I thought looking over some of their work might help."

As they walked toward their cars in the parking lot, Hunter scratched his chin pensively, as he spoke.

"There's something that keeps nagging at a

remote corner of my brain. It has to do with that dollar mark over George Wheeler's picture in the yearbook."

And he said no more.

FOURTEEN

LT. FRANK DISALVO wearily approached the three-story Early American–style building, with its shuttered windows, and red-brick exterior, situated just off posh Washington Square in downtown Philadelphia. As he entered the lobby, he was aware that the air had been conditioned against the continuing May heat wave on this late Wednesday afternoon.

He took the elevator to the third floor where junior partner George Carlisle had his law office. When he stepped off of the elevator, DiSalvo felt he had walked onto the set of what could have been a TV show called "Future Law." Everything was white and chrome. There were computer-modular stations for secretaries and legal assistants placed in front of him in a circular room, which had hallways shooting off in four directions. The various laminated tiers of the work

stations were filled with computer monitors, key-
boards, printers, mini-photocopiers, and fax
machines. The place was noisy, with young men
and women (all wearing communications head-
sets) darting around the room, and up and down
the hallways. High-tech beeps and whirs sounded
everywhere.

After flashing his badge and stating his name,
DiSalvo was escorted by a very sexy, blonde legal
assistant (whose firm, thin body, the policeman
guessed, was fashioned via fitness center aerobic
exercises), to George Carlisle's office. "Office"
was not quite the accurate word—it was more of
a legal game room. There was, to be sure, a wall
filled with books placed in inset, white book-
cases. But there was also an electronic island with
computer gadgets, VCR, DVD, CD and cassette
players, and a large-screen television. There was
a 1950's–style juke box in one corner, next to a
wet bar. In an alcove off to one side of Carlisle's
desk was a weightlifting workout bench. Carlisle
was seated behind his desk, tossing nerf-type bas-
ketballs at a net with a backboard situated against
the wall next to the workout bench. Another very
attractive female, this one brunette, sat in front of

the desk. She held a small audio digital recorder, as Carlisle spoke to her with his back to the doorway where DiSalvo stood.

"Excuse the interruption," said DiSalvo. "I'm Lt. DiSalvo from the Philadelphia Police Department. I made an appointment to see you today."

Carlisle spun around in his chair, looked at DiSalvo, and smiled.

"Well, well. Brown suit," said Carlisle. "I thought, being a cop, you'd be a blue dude."

And right away, DiSalvo knew he was dealing with a wise ass. He ran his smile program.

"I thought it might be better if we could speak alone," the lieutenant said.

Carlisle turned to the woman, and dismissed her by saying, "Why don't you take what I just gave you, and run it up Mr. North's flagpole. Let me know if it goes up higher than half-mast."

After they were alone, Carlisle got up, leaned his lanky body against the bar, and ran his right hand through his Brillo-like hair.

"I know that you are on duty, Lieutenant, but can I offer you any jeopardy-producing potent potables?" asked Carlisle.

"Orange juice would be fine," responded

DiSalvo, as he pulled his pad and pen out of his jacket pocket. "I'm sorry, but I'm afraid I'll be asking you some pretty disturbing questions."

Carlisle handed DiSalvo his orange juice, and sat himself down at his desk with what looked like a Tom Collins. He picked up a nerf ball.

"Fire away," he said, as he shot off the ball at the net.

"Where were you last Saturday morning?" asked DiSalvo.

"Well, Lieutenant," said Carlisle, as he locked the fingers of both hands behind his neck, with his elbows sticking out, "Saturday is part of the weekend. So, I end what I do during the week. I like to sleep late on Saturday. Which is what I was doing in my East River Drive condo. Mother did not approve of this indulgence. She was always up early on weekends, riding horses, working on cases, whatever. I tried to tell her that hard work died a while ago, along with honesty, modesty, and generosity."

"So," said DiSalvo, "it appears that you and your mother did not get along."

"Bingo!" said Carlisle, as he shot off another nerf. "Hey, but don't get me wrong. Her money was always there when I needed it. And in case you're getting any nasty police-like ideas, I want to assure you that I wouldn't have wanted to cash her in since she had quite a few capital years left of future growth."

"Did your mother have any connections with George Wheeler?" asked DiSalvo.

"None that I know of," said Carlisle. "They knew each other because Ronald Wheeler and I are friends. Nothing beyond that."

"What about your mother and Dr. Thomas Bergman?" asked DiSalvo.

"Business or pleasure?" asked Carlisle, with a smirk.

"You tell me," said DiSalvo.

"The good doctor did make house calls," said Carlisle. "But, that was their business, or pleasure. Anyway, it didn't matter to me."

"Where were you on the morning of George Wheeler's death?" asked DiSalvo. At this point, he just wanted to get his answers and leave. He thought that he would prefer the heat outside. It was too cool in here.

"I was on my way here, to—should I say the 'w' word?" asked Carlisle.

"One more thing," said DiSalvo, ignoring the young lawyer's wordplay. "Your father. Is he still in the picture at all?"

"The man who participated in my conception, you mean," said Carlisle. "No. Hardly knew him. He invested as little time as possible in the partnership with my mother. I was my mother's dividend. His assets soared from the merger and subsequent dissolution of the marriage contract with the daughter of General Motor's biggest investor. Fade to black. Too bad he didn't stick around longer. I think I could have learned a great deal from him."

"Speaking of not being able to stick around," said DiSalvo, "I have to run. Thank you for your time, Mr. Carlisle."

Carlisle flipped a nerf ball to DiSalvo, who caught it with one hand.

"Come on, Lieutenant," said Carlisle, "how about a little one-on-one?"

DiSalvo turned toward the door. As he left, he hook-shot the nerf. As the ball floated through the net, he said, "Sorry, but I have to get back to—work."

FIFTEEN

JUST AS WAS THE CASE with George Wheeler's funeral, Elizabeth Carlisle's undertaking was delayed until the weekend to accommodate the arrival of the numerous mourners. However, the ceremony was not at the Carlisle estate. Maxwell Hunter's Volkswagen seemed foreign indeed as he pulled into the Baker Funeral Home parking lot. It looked to him as if every high-priced GM automobile division was represented. Betsy Carlisle's father and his business associates were obviously in attendance, thought Hunter.

He drove past the valet parking attendant, and sandwiched his car between two Cadillacs that were parked in the immense flagstone lot. After he got out of his car, he approached the arched entrance to the funeral home. He noted the huge marble and granite walls of the edifice. He walked through the archway, whose iron and brass gates were swung open for the occasion. Hunter said out loud to himself, "They could show this place on 'Death Styles of the Rich and Famous.'"

He was led into the building through a huge wood-carved door by one of the attendants. Once inside, Hunter saw that he was in a large, round, atrium-style reception hall. The mourners stood in a long, circular line which led to the coffin, which was situated at the hub. Once respects were paid, one followed a straight exit aisle to the outside of the circle. Side-chambers were placed around the circle as off-shoot reception lounges for sitting and mingling.

After walking around a bit, Hunter found DiSalvo, who had given the teacher a call early in the morning to confirm that Hunter would be there. The lieutenant had not discussed any aspects of the investigation on the telephone. Once they were in one of the reception lounges, DiSalvo told Hunter about his interviews with Kelly Bergman and George Carlisle. Hunter, in turn, related James Learner's conversation with Manny Bergman.

"Well," said DiSalvo, "that makes Mrs. Bergman my number one suspect. She was involved with George Wheeler. Maybe he was trying to blackmail her, threatening to tell of the affair unless she used her influence with her husband concerning the drug deal. Or, it's possible he really loved her, and she didn't want a scandal and a messy divorce. And, she could have wanted Betsy Carlisle out of the way if she knew about the affair with her husband. That the affair between Dr. Bergman and the Carlisle woman was confirmed by two people makes it unlikely that it was made up to shift guilt onto someone else."

"I can understand the second motive you are attributing to Mrs. Bergman, but not the first," said Hunter. "If Kelly Bergman knew about her husband's affair, she could have used that knowledge as leverage against her husband if he ever verified her affair. It wouldn't be necessary to kill Wheeler."

"I don't know," said DiSalvo, "she strikes me as a woman who does what she wants, and doesn't want to be found out. I just told you about her possible hospital cover-up."

"Then, what about the strange circumstances at the sites of the murders?" asked Hunter. "The yellow glasses, the ashes on Wheeler's face, the coin in Ms. Carlisle's mouth, and the missing teeth. What are they all about?"

"Just meant to throw us off—make it look as if some kind of psycho is on the loose," replied DiSalvo.

"I don't think so. This all seems too well-planned," said Hunter. "What about Barnum? Any chance he's not telling the truth?"

"He has an alibi," said DiSalvo. "At the exact time of Wheeler's death, based on body temperature of the corpse, the coagulation of the blood on the forehead, the status of the body's organs, and so on, Barnum was seen at a convenience store, where he always stopped in the morning for coffee and a bagel."

"Well," said Hunter, "I'm going to walk around. Maybe I can find some of my ex-students, and talk to them."

"Alright. I'll be here if you need me," said DiSalvo.

Hunter walked to the seats in the main reception section, where the immediate family of the deceased sat. Hunter had never met Mr. Richard Carlisle, Betsy Carlisle's father (Betsy Carlisle had kept her unmarried name, and had insisted that her son carry it on). But, just by looking, he could tell who he was. Mr. Carlisle was an elderly man, probably in his upper sixties, who had kept his good looks. He had a full head of meticulously groomed white hair. His strong, broad shoulders were neatly clothed in a gray, pinstriped jacket. When he was silent, others crowded around him, competing for attention. When he spoke, all of the others stopped what they were doing, and listened. He occasionally gestured, and when this happened, one in the crowd jumped into action, carrying out a decree.

Behind Richard Carlisle's entourage sat the same ex-EFS students that Hunter had seen at the Wheeler funeral. He approached the group of young men.

"I hope we don't have to meet under circumstances like these again," said Hunter. "How are you guys holding up?"

"I'm OK," responded George Carlisle.

"Well, I'm feeling a little shaky," said Daniel Lane. "I find what's happened to be very frightening."

"Pierce, do you have something to relax

Daniel?" asked Hunter, noticing how pale Lane appeared.

"I'm afraid I forgot to bring any medication," said Pierce. "I guess I haven't been thinking too clearly due to the recent events."

As Pierce finished his statement, Hunter noticed his ex-student had not been looking at him, but instead was staring behind Hunter, as if following someone's progress with his eyes.

"What is this?" asked Bergman, as he pointed toward the reception line.

Hunter turned around and recognized another of his former students, Robert Fisher. He was going past the coffin, and heading toward the immediate family.

"What's he doing here?" asked George Carlisle sharply.

"Let's find out, shall we?" said Pierce, and he, Ronald Wheeler, and George Carlisle quickly headed toward Fisher.

"Let's be cool, guys," said Hunter as he re-membered the rivalry and bad feelings between Fisher and some of the well-to-do boys. He quickly recalled how that animosity had been heightened as Robert Fisher became bitter following the death of Fisher's mother early in the fall of senior year. Hunter thought about Mrs. Fisher, who was a widow who owned a debt-ridden grocery store in the blue collar section of Manayunk, and how she was very active at the school, participating in fund-raising events and other school functions. Hunter had spoken with Mrs. Fisher many times, since her only child was one of the teacher's best students. Hunter had sensed that she had wanted her son to feel part of, not alienated from, the world of EFS. She knew that her son was very talented, and had wanted him to have a good future based on a solid education.

After working at a parents' night ceremony, Mrs. Fisher had been walking to her car parked in the Eastwood section, not far from the school, when she was struck by a sports car. Hunter remembered it was a Porsche, apparently stolen from one of the affluent residents of the area by an ex-convict. As far as Hunter knew, the criminal was still serving time for his crimes.

Bergman, Wheeler, and Carlisle worked their way through the crowd and caught up to Fisher at the side entrance to the main reception area.

Hunter arrived there a second later, and heard Bergman talking.

"Well, well," he said, "if it isn't the Fisher. We don't really think that you're here to pay your respects, Reds."

Hunter remembered that Fisher only let people he liked call him Reds, and he was sure Bergman knew this.

"You think right," he said coldly.

"Then why are you here?" asked Wheeler, with a look of disdain.

"Morbid curiosity," responded Fisher, with equal contempt. He smiled, and said, "I wanted to see how the other half died."

"I'm going to get you thrown out of here," said Carlisle to Fisher, and he left.

"You should have let me know you were coming, Reds," said Bergman, looking at Fisher's plain, brown suit. "I could have at least advised you on how to dress. I could have lent you the emerald and gold tie clasp I recently made. Just for the day, of course."

Fisher noticed Hunter.

"Mr. Hunter, I'm disappointed in you," he said. "Why are you soiling yourself with the filthy rich?"

"I'm frightened," said Hunter, "and concerned, because people connected with EFS are dying. That school is your alma mater, too."

"These people," said Fisher with disgust, "showed no concern when *mia mater* was run over by a car. Look at them. They don't mourn like you and I do. They have their cushy world to fall back into after the blow is struck."

"You're in too deep here, Fisher," said Bergman. "Swim back to your small, safe, shallow pond."

Fisher showed his icy smile.

"I'd like nothing better than to get away from you people," he said. "But, maybe, someday, the tide will turn, and we'll be occupying the same waters."

Bergman looked at Fisher, then at Hunter.

"Don't wait for the pendulum to swing your way," he said.

Fisher laughed, and turned to Hunter.

"Some English Lit. student," he said. "He couldn't even carry through the metaphor. I'm out of here."

And with that, he quickly turned away and made his exit.

Bergman and Wheeler walked away without a word, and returned to their seats. Hunter stood where he was, scratching his chin, thinking about what had just happened.

DiSalvo came out of the crowd and approached Hunter.

"What's going on?" asked the lieutenant. "George Carlisle was trying to get somebody thrown out. What gives?"

DiSalvo saw Hunter start to say something, and then stopped.

"Nothing. I have to get out of here. I have to think a little bit. Keep in touch," he said.

And then he left, leaving DiSalvo to scratch his own chin.

SIXTEEN

SATURDAY NIGHT HAD slowly turned into early Sunday at Pierce Bergman's seashore home just outside Margate, New Jersey. Bergman and his friends had arrived late in the day following Betsy Carlisle's funeral. They were all tired and had sprawled out in different parts of the large, sunken living room. Situated around the room were a number of florescent-lit tanks containing all sorts of tropical fish. The light from the tanks bathed the faces of the young men in a ghostly hue.

Bergman had been in the kitchen whipping up drinks for everyone. He came out into the living room area with the refreshments, and handed them out.

"What a gloomy bunch," he said to Daniel Lane, as he served him a Bloody Mary.

Lane stared into his drink, and then took a sip, before speaking.

"I'm worried," he said. "All of this is pretty strange. First Ronald's father, then George's mother. I'm afraid this isn't over, yet."

"Why don't you take a look at this," said Pierce. "It will take your mind off of things."

Bergman walked over to one of the large picture windows, and looked into an expensive-looking telescope situated in front of it.

"At this time of night, you can see quite a heavenly body," he said with a smile.

"Let's have a look-see," said George Carlisle, getting up from his seat.

Ronald Wheeler and Oliver Ford formed a line behind Carlisle. Carlisle looked into the eyepiece and saw a drop-dead gorgeous blonde, who was in the house next to Bergman's. The ceiling-to-floor windows of the bedroom were totally uncovered. The woman was already half-naked, clothed only in a bikini bottom. George started to drool slightly as he stared at her large breasts.

"Please," said Bergman, "you are salivating on the instrument."

"Does she do this often?" asked Carlisle, as he continued to ogle.

"Why, yes, as a matter of fact," responded

Bergman, as he walked to a desk and picked up some photographs that were lying there. He threw them to Lane, who had remained seated. Lane looked at the pictures which depicted a nude woman.

"Infra-red, telephoto lens," said Bergman.

"Oh, boy, she just took off the rest!" said Carlisle.

"Hey, give us a shot!" demanded Wheeler.

Lane turned to Bergman.

"Don't you think this is a little sleazy, Pierce?" he said.

"For us, or for her?" responded Bergman. "Besides, you wrong me. I am only interested in the behavior of yonder maiden. Why does she do this? She doesn't know for sure that someone is looking. She probably would cover those windows immediately if she did. She doesn't want to be a slut, at least not publicly. Yet, she knows how attractive she is. She may be thinking to herself, 'If someone is looking, let them see what they can't have.' It will only make the deprivation worse. And so, maybe she gets a cheap thrill, as does the voyeur. Maybe all day she has to pretend to be a model citizen. Maybe she likes to play at being caught at what she really is, passionate and sexy. It's fascinating, don't you think?"

Daniel Lane got up and walked up the steps leading to the bookcase against a wall above the living room. He looked at the titles on the shelves.

"Don't act so offended, Daniel," said Carlisle. "You were part of some slightly unethical behavior, as were the rest of us, in high school."

"Yeah," said Oliver Ford, "my mother may deal in real estate, but I learned free enterprise with this group."

"Yes, sir, that was a pretty slick operation we had going at EFS, selling cheat sheets and term papers," said Wheeler. "Our networking was pretty extensive at the end, there. We were making some good money when we started buying from, and supplying other schools."

Oliver Ford, after getting his fill of the beauty through the telescope, wandered over to Bergman's laboratory next to the kitchen. He looked into the microscope on the counter, and looked at a slide of some dead insect. He gazed at the sealed bottles in racks which contained various species of deceased and preserved reptiles. He also glanced at the jewelry-making tools on another shelf. He noticed that Bergman had gone back into the kitchen, and had reentered the living room with chips, dip, and microwave popcorn.

"Remember how old Pierce, here, liked to pull jokes on some students," said Ford to the others. "Every once in a while, he would give the wrong answers to one of our customers. He really enjoyed seeing them squirm when they didn't know what to write down at test time."

"I was simply teaching a lesson about dishonesty," said Bergman. "I should be commended. I was showing them that crime did not pay."

"Yeah," laughed Wheeler, "at least not for them."

They all laughed, except for Lane, who continued to look through the book he held, which contained the poems of Edgar Allen Poe.

"Didn't you guys ever feel guilty," asked Lane, "about doing this stuff at the expense of others? Did you ever stop to think about how much the few of us have, and how little so many others have?"

Bergman ignored him.

"Well, my brother, Manny, is carrying on with the enterprise we started," said Bergman, "and, it is doing better than ever."

Bergman walked over to the television and VCR. He opened a teakwood panel on the side of the entertainment unit, and revealed rows of videocassettes. He took one out, and held it up to the others.

"I thought you might enjoy a hidden video on the techniques of my brother, Manny, as he tries to put the moves on a female classmate," said Bergman. He then loaded the tape, turned on the TV and VCR, and sat down with the others as he held the remote control in his hand.

On the screen was Manny, seated on a sofa with an attractive redhead, probably a junior or senior. She wore a clingy yellow top and a short, tight black skirt. Manny looked bug-eyed, and kept staring at the girl's legs, even when she spoke to him. The camera would zoom in on the girl's luscious legs, then cut to Manny's face in a tight close-up. The young men howled with laughter as they watched the tape.

"So, anyway, Daisy," said Manny, "my brother's got this cool place down at the shore. It's got five bedrooms."

At this point, Bergman did some rewinding, and had Manny repeat the "It's got five bedrooms," line again. The others responded with loud cackling. Bergman repeated this action with other lines throughout the tape. Sometimes he slowed the tape down, as he did when the girl uncrossed and then crossed her legs, to accentuate the action. One time he sped up the playback, when Manny unconsciously scratched his crotch. It appeared as if his brother was performing rapid-fire masturbation.

Manny moved close to the girl, and started to touch her hair.

"You know how to win me over, don't you, Manny?" asked Daisy.

"Oh, yeah," said Manny, and he reached into his pocket and pulled out a small jewelry box. He opened it.

"Oh, they're beautiful!" said Daisy, as she reached for the box quickly (rewind and instant replay of greedy grab), and placed gold earrings on her lobes. Manny seized the opportunity, and planted a kiss on the girl's lips, and grabbed her knee with his hand (zoom-in on the hand).

More mundane conversation followed. Then, Manny went in for the kill.

"So, how about you and me at my brother's place?" he asked.

"Well, I don't know," Daisy said, "I think I might need more convincing."

Manny reached into his other pocket and pulled out a long velvet jewelry case. He opened it.

"For you," he said. He took out a sparkling watch, and fastened it on Daisy's wrist. She lit up like a Christmas tree, and threw her arms around Manny. As they embraced, she seemed almost oblivious to Manny as she stared at her bejeweled wrist behind his neck. In the meantime, Manny had placed his hands on the girl's behind, and was squeezing it, lifting up her skirt at the same time.

"So will you come with me to the house?" asked Manny.

(Zoom-in on Manny's hands, and Daisy's wiggling bottom)

"I think," said Pierce Bergman, "we can take that as a 'yes.' I never knew my parents' security system could be put to such good use."

The others, except for Daniel Lane, slapped their knees and laughed.

"I apologize," said Carlisle. "You can show us a good time, Pierce."

Pierce smiled. Daniel Lane, who had stood near the bookcase the whole time that the tape was being played, turned to put the volume of Poe back in its place. He walked to his designated bedroom without a sound and closed the door behind him, cutting himself off from his friends.

SEVENTEEN

THE BLACK SUIT did not fit Maxwell Hunter in more ways than one. He did not like wearing a jacket and tie, and avoided formal affairs whenever possible. Consequently, the suit he was now wearing was an old one. He had put on weight since he had bought it, and the jacket pulled at the waist, and the pants were too tight. He owned a couple of sports jackets, which he wore with an open collar at school functions involving the parents of students. He had not worn ties at the recent funerals he had attended. But, he had decided to dig out his old suit for this year's Eastern Friends School Faculty Ball.

He had dodged going to this affair whenever he had had the chance because he did not like the affluent atmosphere surrounding it. But now, he felt that he should attend all school activities to pick up on anything that might concern the murders. When he had shown up at Patricia's door, she had laughed at his ill-fitting attire. She said his clothes looked as if they had been bought at a funeral director's close-out sale. Hunter looked at Patricia now, and thought that she was stunning in the wine-colored dress that she wore, with her dark brown hair worn up.

It was early Sunday evening, the day after Betsy Carlisle's funeral. The Ball was being held this year at the Franklin House, an elegant banquet hall which bordered on the upscale section of Eastwood, and the poverty-stricken area of Drydock. The banquet hall was surrounded by manicured lawns, with tall brick and iron fencing around the perimeter. There were security cameras and floodlights positioned about the property. The building itself had a domed ceiling. The main entrance, whose only access was at the top of a steep flight of stairs, was flanked by columns. The building was painted white, and trimmed in Williamsburg blue.

Once inside, Hunter felt as if he had entered some rich person's mansion. There were antique furniture pieces all around. Ceiling-to-floor fire-places were placed across from each other in the banquet area. There was a small orchestra playing music. One side of the room had tables filled with champagne, caviar, hors d'oeuvres, baked hams, salads, turkeys, prime rib, and pastries sculpted in various shapes. The most distinctive feature of the room was the series of mirrors hung on the walls, which gave it, what Patricia called, a Palace of Versailles look.

Patricia and Hunter, after eating their main courses, were at the dessert tables when Hunter spotted Lt. DiSalvo standing next to Dr. Falls.

"Come on," Hunter said to Patricia, "let's have a talk with DiSalvo."

They walked to the area in front of the head table where Dr. Falls and DiSalvo stood. They exchanged greetings.

"I was just telling your boss, here," said DiSalvo, "that I think he should have canceled this shindig, given the circumstances. EFS people have been targeted by a maniac, and this place could be where he sets his sights next."

"I told the lieutenant," said Dr. Falls, "that we cannot stop all school functions out of fear. The activities at the end of the school year are important to our students, their parents, our alumni, and teachers. Besides, these violent crimes have taken place in isolation, in rather secluded areas."

"I tend to agree with Dr. Falls, Lieutenant," said Hunter. "I'd be very surprised if our killer struck here, given the circumstances surrounding the previous crimes."

"Sorry," said DiSalvo, not convinced, "I still don't like it."

"There's Mark Henry," said Patricia. "It looks as if he's handing out sheets of paper to the guests."

"Oh, dear," said Dr. Falls, "I have a bad feeling about this. Excuse me, but I'd better go and see what he is passing out."

"I think I can show you that," said DiSalvo, and he pulled one of the sheets out of his jacket pocket. "He handed this to me as I walked in."

Falls took it and read it. The flyer urged those present not to have the Faculty Ball in the future, but instead to donate the fee amount to the school's scholarship fund for needy families who wanted to send their talented children to EFS.

"Well, my job will never get dull with Mark around," laughed Dr. Falls, and he left to talk with Henry.

"I would have handed out flyers myself if I could have gotten this thing canceled today," said DiSalvo with a worried look.

"Lieutenant," said Hunter, "was anything stolen following the funeral yesterday?"

"No, not a thing," answered DiSalvo. "I guess our security was tight enough."

"What's your next move, Lieutenant?" asked Patricia.

DiSalvo ran a hand through his hair, and shrugged his shoulders.

"I don't really know," he said. "Since the children of the two victims went to school together, and are still friends, I figured there's a good chance that a parent of another one in this group of friends could be the next target."

"Sounds very possible to me," said Hunter.

"We also noted that single parents of only children had been killed," continued DiSalvo. "I did some research. One of the boys that you taught, Oliver Ford, fits the pattern. Father was killed in an automobile accident. The mother, Martha Ford, inherited a great deal of real estate, and holds the lease to the Eastern Men's' Athletic Club, which, I understand, has a large number of

EFS alumni. I approached Mrs. Ford about having a police detective stick close by. She didn't want to have any part of it. Said having the law too close was bad for business. But, I'm having squad cars patrol close to her workplace, and her home, at least for the next several weeks. Truth is, I don't have the manpower to tail every possible victim." He paused. "Pick up anything so far at this get-together, Hunter?"

"Only a stuffed stomach," said Hunter.

"That reminds me," said DiSalvo, "next Sunday I'd like to invite both you and Ms. Delvecchio to my parents' house in South Philadelphia for dinner, about 4:00 p.m. My father was born in Italy, Ms. Delvecchio, and he and my mom speak Italian. I promise you an authentic Italian meal."

"Grazie," said Patricia, "I'll bring the Chianti."

The lieutenant smiled, then seemed to notice something over Patricia's shoulder. The smile vanished.

"Excuse me," he said. "One of my men has signaled me. After I talk with him, I'll be back."

He abruptly left Hunter and Delvecchio. Hunter saw DiSalvo go near one of the exits to talk with a man dressed in a dark blue suit. He could have been any one of the parents, except that Hunter noticed a slight bulge near the left armpit. He also wore what appeared to be a hearing aid in his right ear, which Hunter assumed was a radio receiver.

"There's Thomas Bergman," said Patricia, as she nodded toward the buffet table. The doctor was standing next to a tall, attractive, dark-haired woman, who Hunter guessed was in her mid-forties. They were chatting and laughing. The woman looked familiar to Hunter.

"I know who that woman is," said Hunter, remembering. "That's Dolores Lane. She's the mother of Daniel Lane, another one of my ex-students. I haven't seen her in quite a while."

"Well," said Patricia, "Dr. Bergman does not seem to have taken the passing of Ms. Carlisle too badly. And where is the good doctor's wife?"

Hunter looked around and spotted Kelly Bergman at the opposite end of the hall, wearing an ebony evening gown. Mrs. Bergman, along with her husband, had been at many school affairs over the years, so Hunter had no trouble recognizing them. Mrs. Bergman was talking with a broad-shouldered gentleman, whose back was toward Hunter and Delvecchio.

"Over there, near the French windows," he said to Patricia.

"Well," said Patricia, "at least *she* is wearing black."

At that moment, Lt. DiSalvo weaved across the room and stood stone-faced in front of them.

"I have to go," he said. "There's been a shooting. A boy, not far from here, in the Germantown section." He hesitated. "I don't think it has anything to do with the other murders, but, the boy's name is Malcolm Henry. Do you think …?"

"What street?" interrupted Hunter.

"Germantown and Chelten Avenues," answered DiSalvo.

"That's close to where Mark Henry lives," said Hunter softly. "I'll tell Henry, Lieutenant, and we'll both go with you. Patricia, you stay here and keep an eye on things. Let us know if you see anything unusual."

DiSalvo heard the determined sound in Hunter's voice, and knew that this was a courageous act for the teacher. Going to the scene of an urban murder was obviously not an easy thing for Hunter to do.

"Go and get Henry," said DiSalvo. "I'll be waiting outside."

And with that, he quickly left.

EIGHTEEN

IT WAS DUSK, when things do not look quite right. It was the time of day when the world does not seem clear. The eyes are not ready yet for the night, and there is not enough light to see what is really going on.

Hunter looked at Mark Henry, who was seated to his right in the back seat of Lt. DiSalvo's Taurus. Henry stared straight ahead. His right hand was squeezing the arm rest tightly. When Hunter had told him about the shooting, Henry seemed to freeze. His back became stiff, and all the muscles in his face tightened up. It literally looked as if Mark Henry was trying to pull himself together. The only thing Henry had said after hearing the news was that Malcolm Henry was his nephew. Now, in the car, he looked like a person trying to hold on, and the arm rest had to do.

It started to rain, light, but steady. The car approached an intersection. There were police cars there. A crowd of people stood around the blocked-off area. Uniformed policemen stood around the crowd, keeping the people away from the center of the scene. DiSalvo flashed his badge to one of the policemen, and they were waved through. The lieutenant parked next to one of the police cars. DiSalvo told Hunter and Henry to wait in the car until he returned. He got out of his car, and walked over to the policeman who stood nearby. They talked for several minutes. DiSalvo walked back to his car.

"Mr. Henry," said DiSalvo quietly, "we would like you to confirm the identity of the boy."

Henry slowly moved his head, looked at the lieutenant, blinked, as if coming out of a trance, and gradually got out of the car. Hunter followed the other two as they walked to the clearing in the intersection.

The blacktop glistened in the misty rain. Malcolm Henry was sprawled out in the street. To Hunter, he looked as if he was frozen in the act of running, cut down in mid-stride. His left arm was bent behind him, where the red of his blood spread over the black surface of the road. His right arm, also bent at the elbow, was in front of him, the hand almost at face level. The upper part of the body was thrust forward. The left leg was straight; the right, bent at the knee, as if ready to push off once more. Malcolm was smartly dressed in black and red, from the cap on his head, to the sneakers on his feet.

"Is this your nephew, Mr. Henry?" asked DiSalvo.

"Yes," said Mark Henry quickly.

"How old … was he?" asked the lieutenant.

"Sixteen," responded Henry.

"How can we contact the boy's mother and father?" continued DiSalvo.

"We don't know where the father is," said Henry as he stopped looking at the boy. "His mother, my sister, never married the father. She lives about three blocks from here. It was her turn to work at the department store this weekend. I'll go with you to tell her what happened."

The ambulance had arrived. Henry walked with Hunter to the side of the street, near the crowd. They heard some of the neighborhood kids talking behind them.

"It's a damn shame," said one girl.

"Yeah," agreed a boy, "but he went out looking decent."

"Damn straight," said another boy. "Those Nike Airs look cool."

"How about that LRG zip hoody and fitted hat? Proper," said another.

"Those pants are bad. Rocawear for sure," said one of the girls.

"And those shades!" echoed another. "They're slammin'."

DiSalvo rejoined them as the first boy spoke again.

"That's all we can really hope for, isn't it? To go out lookin' good."

"Your nephew apparently was accosted by other youths," DiSalvo said, deciding to keep it impersonal. "They wanted certain items of apparel. He refused, and bolted. They shot him in the back, and ran when too many people showed up."

There was a pause.

"That's all they can really hope for, isn't it?" repeated Henry quietly. "To go out looking good."

He paused, and walked closer to the kids. He

addressed Hunter and DiSalvo, as if speaking for the neighborhood.

"Malcolm had his precious things, just like rich people. He wanted fine things, just like rich people. He wanted status, as do others. But, he could only afford a few things. And, he worked after school every day to buy them. Those who killed him were trying the easy way to get those few precious things. The wrong way. But greed rolls downhill, too, you know, from the top of the money chain to here. But if the rich lose one day, they just buy the next ten to make up for it. But these kids do not have anything to fall back on. They don't have yesterday, or tomorrow. The past holds nothing but pain, and the future no hope for anything different. All they have is today. And most just want to live for now, no matter if it's just for a moment, no matter what the cost."

Henry stopped and looked as his nephew was taken into the ambulance.

"I'll take you to my sister now, Lieutenant," he said.

After he spoke, Mark Henry walked toward DiSalvo's car, as the rain began to fall hard.

NINETEEN

THE RAIN THAT HAD started on Sunday continued into the week. Maxwell Hunter sat on the sofa in the living room of his house, and listened to the rain hitting the window on this Wednesday evening. He had a stack of test bluebooks piled next to him. He finally had been successful in unearthing the final examinations of the students he taught ten years ago.

As he read the essays, he realized how long it had been since he had taught classes on American Literature. He had taught it the first couple of years at EFS, but had been reassigned to teach British and Comparative Literature. He came to prefer the foreign writers and felt more at home reading their works. As time went by, it was America that felt like a foreign country to him.

He read the essays of his former students. The evil of the woods in *The Scarlet Letter* turned into the horror of the city in Sister Carrie. Then, the West and the frontier were romanticized in the works of other later writers. He read essays by George Carlisle on *Moby Dick,* by Pierce Bergman on Edgar Allen Poe, by Robert Fisher on Ernest Hemingway and F. Scott Fitzgerald, and by Daniel Lane on Sinclair Lewis and John Steinbeck.

He not only read what they had written, but Hunter also paid attention to every detail of their writing. Most of the tests were written in blue, ball-point ink. Some were in black. George Carlisle wrote with a black flair pen. Pierce had used a peacock-blue felt tip, and Daniel Lane was the only one to write in red ink. Since the standard color of choice for corrections by teachers was red, Hunter remembered he had had to switch to a different-colored ink to correct Lane's papers.

But, the bluebook he kept coming back to was Fisher's. It was written in ball-point green ink. Hunter stared at the color, and slowly shook his head from side to side.

TWENTY

THAT FRIDAY, AS THEY did almost every Friday, George Carlisle and Ronald Wheeler walked together toward their cars in the underground parking lot of the Eastern Men's Athletic Club after their workout. The two would usually be the earliest among their group of friends to arrive, since they wanted to leave early to get a jump on the start of the weekend. While they walked, Carlisle was talking, with his head turned toward Wheeler. As they approached the attorney's reserved parking space, Wheeler stared straight ahead, and realized that space was all that was there in front of them.

"George," said Wheeler, "did you drive over here today?"

"What do you mean?" said Carlisle, "I always drive over here from the east side. I wouldn't be caught dead taking public transportation."

"Then, what happened to your car?" asked Wheeler.

They both stared at the empty parking space. Carlisle's new green Porsche was gone.

TWENTY-ONE

ATLANTIC CITY WAS ONE of the last places Lt. Frank DiSalvo expected to be at 3:00 a.m. on Saturday morning, one week after Betsy Carlisle's funeral. He had unexpectedly started working this graveyard shift when he received George Carlisle's phone call just before the lieutenant was ready to leave work for home. He and Hunter had previously spread the word throughout the EFS community to report directly to DiSalvo anything stolen following the theft of Ronald Wheeler's laptop computer.

When he found out about Carlisle's sports car, DiSalvo initiated an APB, and instituted a full departmental search for the Porsche. He also had his people contact all municipal police departments which could have been within driving distance of Philadelphia from the time that Carlisle parked his car to the time it was reported stolen.

Later, during the night, DiSalvo learned that the Atlantic City Police Department had found the car. What the ACPD had not expected to find was what was inside the Porsche. As DiSalvo got out of his Taurus at Bridge St. and Pacific Ave., at the southern end of Atlantic City, he approached the Porsche with a sense of dread.

The lieutenant held up his badge as he walked between the variously parked police cars with their flashers on, and through the crowd of policemen.

"Absolutely nothing has been touched, per your instructions," said a sergeant.

"Thank you," said DiSalvo. He looked inside the Porsche. What he saw gave him the shivers. A lifeless form sat at the wheel. It was a woman in a nightgown. There was a large blood stain under her left breast. In her hands was a melted down, unlit wax candlestick. But the strangest part of the macabre scene was what appeared to be a brown grocery bag placed over the head of the victim.

DiSalvo pulled away from the window and circled the sports car. He noticed another odd detail to add to the list. The left, rear wheel of the car had a black circle painted around the sidewall of the tire. DiSalvo talked to the lieutenant from the Atlantic City Police Department who was in charge. After their discussion, photographs from every angle were taken of the scene. After this was accomplished, DiSalvo, with plastic gloves on his hands, lifted the bag off of the woman. The Atlantic City lieutenant aimed his flashlight at the face of the victim. Her nose was swollen and distorted, and blood had splashed down on the chin.

"Do you know who she is?" he asked DiSalvo.

Despite the bruise, DiSalvo recognized the corpse. He had studied photographs, and had met many of the parents of EFS students and alumni. He had encountered this woman at the Faculty Ball the previous Sunday, when she was introduced as Daniel Lane's mother.

"Yes," said DiSalvo, "her name is Dolores Lee Lane."

TWENTY-TWO

Lt. Frank DiSalvo knew he had been a bad host. He had let his parents carry out the social functions at this Sunday dinner, which included Maxwell Hunter and Patricia Delvecchio. DiSalvo was dead tired. He had not returned to his office until the middle of Saturday, and had started investigating alibis of various suspects. He made telephone calls, along with members of his staff, and had sent out officers to contact those who could be involved. At the same time, he was on standby for any word from the Atlantic City Police Department. He had finally collapsed into his bed early Sunday morning.

DiSalvo took another sip of espresso, hoping it would give him a jolt of alertness. He watched as Patricia and Hunter helped his mother clear the table following the meal. DiSalvo had not met his dinner guests prior to arriving at his parents' house, and had not, as of yet, briefed Hunter on the details surrounding Dolores Lane's death. So, whatever the English teacher knew, he had heard from the media.

DiSalvo looked at Hunter, and saw that he had not taken the news well. He had not spoken much during dinner, and DiSalvo's mother kept saying how pale Hunter looked. The English teacher now sat, his body looking caved in, in the easy chair placed at the end of the sofa in the living room. The lieutenant sat in a rocker at the other end of the sofa, next to the coffee table. DiSalvo's father sat on the sofa. He was a broad-shouldered, rugged-looking man, with a full head of gray hair. He had alert eyes and a warm smile.

"So, Mr. Hunter," said Mr. DiSalvo, "do you get a chance to come to this neighborhood often?"

Hunter, who seemed to be lost in thought, realized he had been asked a question when he saw the elder DiSalvo staring at him.

"Sorry," he said, "what did you say?"

"Do you get down here often?" Mr. DiSalvo repeated.

"No, I'm sorry to say," said Hunter. "I have gone to the Italian Market on Ninth Street many times, but I haven't really walked around the streets much. It seems like a nice place to live."

Mr. DiSalvo leaned back, raised his right arm and rested it on the back of the sofa, and seemed to stare at the electric light on the end table.

"It's not bad," he said. "I've lived here since I was a child. My mother and father brought me to the United States from Italy when I was a baby. When we first arrived, we lived in a house only one block from here. My father worked in a hat factory. My brother worked as a butcher. Me, I worked for the Federal Government, until I retired. Oh, before I worked for the Government, I had a lot of jobs: laborer, bartender, milkman. Also, there were my four years in the Army in World War II. This neighborhood holds a lot of memories: kids growing up, playing ball; men and women of all faiths, trying to get through the Depression."

He stopped for a minute to look at his son.

"When Frankie was growing up," he continued, "everyone would sit outside on the front door steps, or beach chairs in the summer. People would talk about sports, or politics. Kids would harmonize to music played on the radio. One night a week, a family would invite the whole block over for hot Texas wieners bought at a store on Fifteenth Street, or for Chinese food. The next week, another family would volunteer to be the hosts. Some people would fall asleep outside on their beach chairs at night. People didn't lock their doors."

He paused.

"Now? Now, I don't see the neighbors much. Everybody seems to be busy, or tired. I don't even know half of them. They all stay inside most of the time. Doors are always locked. I don't know what's going on anymore."

Lt. DiSalvo got up, gave his father a warm smile, and turned to Hunter.

"Come on," he commanded. "Let's go outside and sit on the step. I have to tell you a few things."

DiSalvo and Hunter went outside and sat on the brown steps of the row house. It was a beautiful, warm spring day, without a cloud in the sky. DiSalvo waited for Hunter to start speaking. Finally, the teacher spoke.

"Alright," he said, "let me have it."

DiSalvo related the grisly details surrounding Dolores Lane's death. Hunter just stared ahead, revealing no emotion. After DiSalvo was finished, there was a short silence.

"Dolores Lee Lane. Her nickname was Dolly," said Hunter. "What do you know about her?"

"She was rich," said DiSalvo, "like the others. She came from a family which made its fortune in oil. She's been divorced for quite a while, now. Ex-husband is in advertising, and lives in New York. We're checking on him. Ms. Lane's parents said he never comes to Philadelphia. Dolores Lane owned a beach house not far from Atlantic City. Apparently, she liked the casino scene. From what I've gathered so far, she was a real party animal."

DiSalvo waited for Hunter to say something, but he did not.

"We were wrong about the next victim," said the lieutenant, sadly. "Daniel Lane has a sister, named Miranda. She is currently in a mental institution. She has been declared legally incompetent to handle funds. So, I guess there goes our only-child theory."

Hunter was about to say something, when Mr. DiSalvo came to the door.

"Telephone, Frankie. A.C. Police," he said.

The lieutenant and Hunter both went back inside. DiSalvo went to the telephone in the living room. Hunter joined Patricia and Mrs. DiSalvo in the kitchen. Patricia was speaking.

"My father," she said, "worked for the United Nations. We traveled a great deal. We spent many years in France and Italy. My mother was an art history scholar, and she taught in Europe."

"My husband and I have been talking about visiting Italy," said Mrs. DiSalvo. "We haven't been there in a long time. But, I am almost afraid that if we go again, we may not want to come back."

She paused.

"So," said Mrs. DiSalvo, "I hope you two enjoyed the meal."

"It was wonderful," said Patricia. "The tortellini in brodo was the best I have had since I tasted it in Rome."

"And, that was the best veal scaloppini I have ever eaten," said Hunter.

"I'm glad to hear that. I love to cook," said Mrs. DiSalvo, "and nothing makes me happier than to see people enjoy a meal. Cooking and eating are very important parts of life, here. A good meal brings people together. It's hard to fight with someone eating at the same table with you."

Lt. DiSalvo entered the kitchen.

"You have a wise mother," said Hunter.

"I know," said DiSalvo, "she reminds me of that fact every day." He smiled at his mother, and then turned back to Hunter.

"I have something else to tell you …" he said, but he was cut off by Hunter.

"Why don't you take a ride with Patricia and me? We're meeting my student, James Learner, at Corner's Bookstore downtown. We can have something at the espresso bar, there."

Hunter looked at Patricia, and then turned back to DiSalvo.

"We have something to tell you, too," he said.

TWENTY-THREE

HUNTER'S CAR HAD DIED on him, again. They rode in Patricia's Peugeot. As they drove toward the center of the city, DiSalvo spoke.

"The ACPD have really jumped on this one. They said it appears that Ms. Lane was killed at her beach house. There were no signs of forced entry, which means she probably knew the killer, and had let him, or her, inside. But, in the bedroom, there were signs of a bit of a struggle. A lamp was knocked over, and objects that had probably been on the dresser were found on the floor. Ms. Lane's blood was found on the sheets and pillow. There was also some vomit and mucus on the pillow. The victim's left breast had been cut on the underside with a knife. But, it did not appear that this was a fatal wound. Neither the heart, nor any main artery had been slit. The breast itself was apparently the object of the incision, as if the murderer wanted it mutilated. Actually, it looks as if she was smothered by the pillow, and the breast was cut later."

"About what time did the murder take place?" asked Hunter.

"Hard to tell," said DiSalvo, "but it looks like sometime shortly after midnight."

"So, where was everybody?" asked Hunter.

"Good question," sighed DiSalvo. "Dr. Thomas Bergman said he was home alone. His wife was supposed to be at a party at a neighbor's house. We called the neighbor, but, although Kelly Bergman had been there, the neighbor could not say when she had left. Manny Bergman said he had been at a party, and when he came home, he thought his parents were asleep. So, he just went to bed. Pierce Bergman was doing overnight work, as he did sometimes on Friday nights. His car was observed in its reserved parking place at the hospital. The young doctor was seen at the hospital, but his presence could not be accounted for during the entire night."

"What about George Carlisle and Ronald Wheeler?" asked Patricia.

"They both said they were alone in their

homes," said DiSalvo. "Ronald Wheeler gave Carlisle a ride after we were done with him concerning the stolen car. Oliver Ford said he was taking care of some business at the Eastern Men's Athletic Club."

"Since you said that Carlisle arrived early at the athletic club, someone could have stolen his car, and parked it someplace else for later use," observed Hunter. "If it were Carlisle himself, he could have not driven to the club, parked it in a lot, walked over to the club, reported the car stolen, picked it up later, and driven to the seashore."

"True," said DiSalvo.

"What about Daniel Lane?" asked Hunter.

"I visited him myself, yesterday," replied DiSalvo. "He acted very strangely. He showed no emotion. He almost looked catatonic. He mumbled something crazy about at least now he no longer had to worry that his mother would be next. He also said he was by himself on Friday night."

"What about the Porsche itself. Any vandalism?" asked Hunter.

"Yeah, as a matter of fact," said DiSalvo.

"Computer processing units and fuses were removed, so the car wasn't going anywhere once it had been parked where it was found. The dashboard was smashed, and the interior was sliced up pretty good."

Patricia pulled into a parking space a couple of blocks from the bookstore. They got out of the car, and Hunter fed the meter enough quarters to last a couple of hours. They started walking. The side of the church building they passed was covered with graffiti. Many stores were not open late on Sunday afternoon, and there were bars covering many of the closed storefronts. They walked through Rittenhouse Square, off of which stood high rise buildings which contained some of the most expensive condominiums in the city. Hunter remembered that when he was growing up, this section of the city was the center of high society. In the Sixties, it was the scene of anti-Vietnam War protests and folk concerts. Now, the wealthy were still here, but the square itself was populated by homeless people, who were sprawled out on the ground, or on the benches. The patchwork of their clothes intermingled with the colors of the flowers, the trees and the grass.

"So," said DiSalvo, as they were walking through the square, "you said that you had to tell me something."

"You first, Pat," said Hunter.

"I was on the phone a great deal today, after the news broke about the Lane killing," she said. "Mostly, people were calling me. Some of the press must have acquired the names of the school's teachers, and started contacting people who worked at EFS, asking if they knew anything. Max got calls, too. Of course, we said nothing. But parents of students and ex-students also called. A great deal of gossip was tossed around. And, I heard, more than once, some dirt about Dolly Lane."

"OK, what gives?" asked DiSalvo quickly. At this point, he was impatient for anything.

"Well, I heard that she had had an affair with George Wheeler," Patricia said.

DiSalvo looked as if he were ready to slap the cuffs on someone.

"That just makes Kelly Bergman stand out even more in my eyes as the number one suspect," he said. "She was involved with the first victim, who was fooling around with the third. And, her husband was getting it on with the second. Love, sex, and jealousy have always been strong motives for murder."

"Cool off," said Hunter. "Don't go busting down any doors yet. Let's go in, get some coffee, and talk first."

They entered Corner's Book Store. Hunter found James Learner near the magazine and newspaper racks on the first floor, where he had told the student to wait for them. Hunter had set up this meeting to review Learner's independent study on American Gothic Fiction, before Dolly Lane's death. After they exchanged greetings, they went up a spiral ramp to the second level and sat at a table at the espresso bar. They ordered espresso and cappuccino, and sipped quietly for a moment, as they watched the customers weave through the book stacks. Hunter spoke first.

"James," he said, "have you heard anything else concerning this nasty business at school?"

"Not really," answered Learner. Hunter thought that he was acting a little shy in front of the lieutenant. Learner took a sip of his cappuccino, and then said, "Manny Bergman likes to talk a lot, though. Mostly about girls and money. He told me that the real wealth in his family comes from his mother's side. But his mother hates managing the money, and she let Manny's father take care of the financial matters early on in the marriage. There have been some fights about money lately, though."

"Yeah," said DiSalvo, "concerning any shares involving George Wheeler, and Betsy Carlisle, no doubt."

"That's all I have," said Learner.

"I do think that money, and wealth, have a lot to do with what's going on here," said Hunter.

"Come on," said DiSalvo, "say what you mean." The lieutenant had a feeling. "Are you trying to protect someone?"

Hunter, feeling found out, proceeded slowly.

"Lieutenant, do you remember at Betsy Carlisle's wake, that you asked me, just before I left, if George Carlisle was trying to get somebody thrown out?"

"Yeah," remembered DiSalvo.

"Well, I wasn't totally honest with you," he said. "There was someone there, an ex-student, who had attended EFS at the same time as the other boys. He never got along well with the others. His name is Robert Fisher. His nickname is Reds."

"So, were these guys enemies?" asked DiSalvo.

Hunter proceeded to tell DiSalvo and Learner about Fisher's past, including the details about his mother's death. Hunter had already told Patricia about Fisher's presence at the funeral.

"After the Carlisle wake," Hunter said, "I thought about Fisher's history, and this old animosity among the boys. But, Lieutenant, when you told me about Dolly Lane's death, I felt a responsibility to tell you about Fisher. There were too many coincidences. The deaths of the mothers of both Fisher and Lane involved Porsches. There was also the grocery bag over Dolly Lane's head. Fisher's mother owned a grocery store, and Reds, an only child, worked there to help his mother, who was a single parent."

Hunter paused. Patricia looked at him.

"There is one more thing," she said softly. "Tell him, Max."

"I also thought about that green dollar mark in the EFS yearbook found in George Wheeler's lap," said Hunter. "I was looking over old test booklets. Robert Fisher was the only student I taught back then who used green ink."

"I'm going to round my men up," said DiSalvo rising from his chair, forgetting all about Kelly Bergman at this point.

"Wait, Lieutenant!" said Patricia. "You don't know Fisher, as we did. We find it inconceivable that he could have committed these murders."

"That's what people always say about these killers," said DiSalvo. "They're very good at hiding their true selves."

"You're forgetting one thing, Lieutenant," said Hunter.

"And what's that?" asked DiSalvo.

"Motive," said Hunter.

"I've got plenty of motive, here," said DiSalvo. "Lower-middle class boy from a working neighborhood, really better than the rest of his classmates at studies and sports, who is looked down upon because of the station in life into which he was born, and who loses his mother while he is still young. He has resentment and a desire for revenge boiling inside him all these years against those who made him and his mother struggle. Why, I've seen a lot less to cause someone to go psycho and start killing. You yourself said money was important, here."

"Yes," said Hunter, "and the killer has given the victims' children more of it."

"Don't you see," continued Patricia, "by taking away the parents of those he despised, Fisher would also be handing his enemies inherited wealth."

"The boys involved," said Hunter, "do not have to share their wealth with anyone. No mother or father, and no siblings are involved. Even Daniel Lane's sister had been declared legally incompetent to handle funds. Oh, this killer is crafty. He probably thought we would be thinking about Oliver Ford as an only child. But, Lane was essentially in the same situation."

DiSalvo, looking disgusted, slowly sank back into his chair.

"You know," said Learner, "this stuff kind of sounds schizophrenic. I mean, wanting to take away kids' parents, but also, giving them money. And, there's also what the lieutenant said about murderers hiding their inner selves. I guess I've been studying Gothic fiction too much. But, it sounds like that stuff about the double nature of things, good versus evil, and all that."

Hunter seemed to be thinking about something, sipping cappuccino, and half-listening to Learner.

"Well," said Hunter to Learner, "you know the double thing isn't only Gothic. It's in modern literature, too. There is the desire in some literature for the author to reflect back on himself, in the absence of a belief in an objective reality. You have Marlow and Jim, in *Lord Jim,* Jake Barnes and Robert Cohn, in *The Sun Also Rises,* Nick Carraway and Jay Gatsby …"

Hunter stopped speaking, and stared wide-eyed at the others.

"Oh my God!" he said, "I've been so stupid! Lieutenant, what color eyes did George Wheeler have?"

DiSalvo quickly reached into his sports jacket pocket for his notebook. He flipped through some pages.

"Ah," he said, "let's see. I've got some notes from the Medical Examiner's office. Here it is. Blue. They were blue. Why?"

"Come on," Hunter said, as he quickly rose from the table, and darted for the spiral walkway. The surprised others followed. Hunter bounded onto the walkway and moved quickly up it. When he reached the third floor of the store, he stopped for an instant, and looked around. He then ran off again.

"What's he doing?" called DiSalvo to Delvecchio, on the run. Patricia just shook her head in response.

Hunter stopped at the book stacks labeled "American Fiction." He started looking quickly through the shelves. He stopped at a book and pulled it off the shelf. At that point, the others caught up with him.

"What the hell is going on, Hunter?" demanded DiSalvo.

Hunter looked around. The store was set up to be very accommodating to customers who wanted to stay for long periods of time. There were comfortable chairs and even tables scattered about the bookstore. Hunter spotted a round table with some empty chairs nearby, and led the others to it. After they sat down, Hunter revealed the book he was holding. It was *The Great Gatsby,* by F. Scott Fitzgerald. Hunter flipped through the pages, and stopped.

"Listen to this," he said, and he began to read from the novel:

The eyes of Doctor T. J. Eckleburg are blue and gigantic—their retinas are one yard high. They look out of no face, but, instead, from a pair of enormous yellow spectacles which pass over a non-existent nose.

Hunter stopped reading and said, "Large, yellow eyeglasses were found on George Wheeler, who had blue eyes."

Patricia seemed to visibly shiver. DiSalvo rubbed his face with his hand. Learner just stared.

"Dr. T. J. Eckleburg is an advertisement sign for an oculist in Fitzgerald's story," explained Hunter. "It is placed in a kind of wasteland area between West Egg, where Gatsby lives, and New York City. Listen to the way Fitzgerald describes this area."

Hunter resumed reading:

This is a valley of ashes—a fantastic farm where ashes grow like wheat into ridges and hills and grotesque gardens.

Hunter paused, and then said, "In the same passage, there are references to 'ash-gray men' in this 'valley of ashes.' Lieutenant—the ashes found on Wheeler's face."

DiSalvo looked at Hunter.

"Good work, Max," he said quietly. He paused, and then said, "There's more, isn't there?"

Hunter nodded his head sadly.

TWENTY-FOUR

JAMES LEARNER LEFT to buy more coffee from the espresso bar. Patricia took three more copies of *The Great Gatsby* from the shelf. Hunter was looking through his copy of the book, and was writing down notes with a pen and some paper Learner had given him.

Learner returned with the coffee about ten minutes later. As he placed the mugs on the table, DiSalvo began to speak.

"I can't emphasize too much how important it is to keep what we're discussing here among ourselves. That especially goes for you, James. I know that you're young, but on this one, you're going to have to act like a very responsible adult."

"I understand," said the student, who was uncharacteristically dead serious on this afternoon.

"You have anything else for us yet, Max?" asked DiSalvo.

"Yes," replied Hunter. "Since we all have the same edition of the novel, please turn to page fifty-four. Lieutenant, in *Gatsby,* Jay Gatsby tries to win back his old girlfriend, Daisy, who has married Tom Buchanan. Daisy's peculiar voice is mentioned in the book. On this page, Gatsby tells the narrator of the story, Nick Carraway, what the voice sounds like." Hunter read aloud:

'She's got an indiscreet voice,' I remarked. 'It's full of—' I hesitated.

'Her voice is full of money,' he said suddenly.

That was it. I'd never understood before. It was full of money—that was the inexhaustible charm that rose and fell in it, the cymbals' song of it. High in a white palace the king's daughter, the golden girl.

Hunter stopped reading.

"Betsy Carlisle was a rich woman," he said, "from a rich family. She became even richer as a lawyer, and her voice was an important instrument in the pursuit of her career. And—she was found dead with a coin placed in her mouth."

Hunter paused as the others read over the passage.

"Lieutenant," he said, "what types of teeth were removed from Ms. Carlisle's mouth? Front? Back? Eye teeth? Molars?"

DiSalvo again looked through his notebook.

"They were both molars," he said.

"Please turn to page thirty-four," Hunter said. "Nick Carraway is talking to a gangster named Meyer Wolfsheim, whom Gatsby knows. Wolfsheim supposedly 'fixed' the 1919 World Series. Wolfsheim is the first to speak." Hunter read to them again:

'I see you're looking at my cuff buttons.'

I hadn't been looking at them, but I did now. They were composed of oddly familiar pieces of ivory.

'Finest specimens of human molars,' he informed me.

There was silence for a short time.

DiSalvo rubbed his chin, and said, "I'll be damned."

"Are you OK?" Delvecchio asked Learner

softly. Beads of perspiration had formed on the boy's forehead.

"Yeah," spat out Learner. "It's just that this is really weird. I mean, it's one thing when it's just a story. It's something else again when this stuff is really happening."

DiSalvo patted the student on the back and gave him a reassuring smile.

"What about Dolly Lane, Max?" asked Di-Salvo.

"Page nine," said Hunter. He felt as if he were conducting one of his classes. "Nick Carraway is kidding Daisy about people missing her in Chicago:

'Do they miss me?' she cried ecstatically.

'The whole town is desolate. All the cars have the left rear wheel painted black as a mourning wreath...'

"There's no doubt about it!" said DiSalvo. "The murderer is taking this stuff right out of the book. The left rear wheel of George Carlisle's Porsche had a black circle of paint on it."

"There's more," said Hunter, in an excited

voice. "Page twenty. Tom Buchanan has a mistress named Myrtle. In a scene where they are together, Tom tells her not to mention his wife, Daisy, anymore. Myrtle had been repeating Daisy's name." Hunter read:

Making a short deft movement, Tom Buchanan broke her nose with his open hand.

"Dolly Lane's nose was broken," said Hunter, "and, her left breast was mutilated. In Gatsby, Myrtle is later killed when she is run over by Gatsby's car, which was actually driven by Daisy at the time. Listen to part of the description of Myrtle's body after being hit by the car. Page sixty-two:

…they saw that her left breast was swinging loose like a flap…

Hunter paused.

"There's one more scene that's particularly disturbing," continued Hunter, reluctantly. He looked at Patricia. "Page fifty-nine. Buchanan is talking to

Gatsby, saying how Gatsby is not good enough for Daisy, and never was." He read again from his book:

I can't speak about what happened five years ago, because I didn't know Daisy then—and I'll be damned if I see how you got within a mile of her unless you brought groceries to the back door.

Hunter slowly looked up from his book, glanced at Patricia, and then looked at DiSalvo.

"As I stated before," the teacher said, "Reds Fisher's mother owned a grocery store at which her son often worked. Dolly Lane was found with a grocery bag placed over her head. And, after looking over old test books, I remembered that Fisher's favorite writer was—F. Scott Fitzgerald."

TWENTY-FIVE

IT WAS GETTING LATE, so Hunter suggested that they go to his place, where he had a special copy of *The Great Gatsby,* complete with critical essays. Lt. DiSalvo bought a copy of the novel, since he did not own one. They gave DiSalvo a lift to his car. James Learner and Hunter rode in Patricia's car. On the way to Hunter's townhouse, there was not much conversation in the Peugeot. They were all thinking.

When both cars arrived at Hunter's home, the English teacher went to fetch his copy of the book, while the others sat down in the living room. Hunter returned, and DiSalvo had a question for him.

"Max, I've been out of school for a while," he said, "and literature was not my best subject. I'm going to have to play a little catch-up here. You want to fill me in a little on *The Great Gatsby?*"

Hunter already had his nose buried in the book as he entered the room.

"Huh?" he grunted. "Oh, ah, James, show us some of your knowledge. Update Lt. DiSalvo, will you?"

Learner ran his right hand through his short-cropped dark brown hair, and said, "The book is, among other things, an indictment of the rich, especially the old, established rich families. The Buchanans, Tom and Daisy, represent that wealth in the book. Gatsby is *nouveau riche,* and he was only able to rise up through dishonest means, such as doing business with gangsters. The way in which the working class is used, and, I guess, abused, by the upper class is depicted by what happens to Myrtle Wilson. Also, Tom rigs it so that Myrtle's husband, George, thinks that Gatsby was Myrtle's lover. Wilson kills Gatsby, and then commits suicide. So, the Buchanans get away scot-free, so to speak."

Patricia laughed at the pun.

"Good form," she said.

"So, we were right from the start," said DiSalvo. "This is about the lower class versus the upper class. And this fellow, Fisher, seems to have turned this struggle into a deadly one."

"Slow down, Lieutenant," said Hunter.

"Why?" asked DiSalvo. "Look at what we have. This guy was treated badly at school by rich kids, who made him feel that he didn't even deserve to attend the same school with them. His mother was a single, struggling parent, killed by a Porsche. Dolly Lane was found dead in a Porsche. You said his favorite author in school was Fitzgerald, and we have established the *Gatsby* connection to details at the crime sites. The book fits right in with his anger toward the wealthy. I think I better bring this Fisher in."

"Do you have any really hard evidence that shows that Fisher committed these crimes?" asked Hunter. "Do you have fingerprints, or eyewitnesses placing him at the scenes of the crimes?"

"No," admitted DiSalvo, "but the coincidences are too numerous to dismiss."

"There are still a few items that do not fit into this overall scheme," said Hunter.

"Like what?" asked DiSalvo.

"That Pluto doll found on Wheeler's car seat," said Hunter. "That's obviously not in the book. What in the world does that represent? Also, that ditch in which Betsy Carlisle was found. Did it look as if it had been there before? Had workers been doing some maintenance on the grounds that had caused it to be there?"

"No," answered DiSalvo, "the staff had not seen it previously. The earth appeared to have been freshly dug."

"What about the size?" asked Hunter. "Was the hole a great deal smaller or bigger than Ms. Carlisle's body?"

"It seemed to be just the right size," said the lieutenant.

"Like an open grave," said Patricia.

"A car winds up in a ditch after an accident following one of Gatsby's parties," noted Hunter.

"Well, there you go," said DiSalvo.

"But, there is no real significance being placed on the ditch in the story," said Hunter. "It's the car accident that holds meaning for us, given Mrs. Fisher's manner of death. And, that connection was made with the Porsche."

"So, we have a redundant killer," said DiSalvo.

"And, what about the broken watch on Betsy Carlisle?" said Hunter. "There's also that candlestick in Dolly Lane's hands. I'm pretty sure they are not in the book."

"Well," said DiSalvo, not wanting to give in, "maybe you just have to give it a closer read. They may show up."

"Perhaps," said Hunter doubtfully. "I'll double-check. Give me a little time here." He resumed his investigation of the story.

"I know," said Patricia, "let's play 'Situations'."

"What's that?" asked DiSalvo.

"Oh, you'll like it, Lieutenant," said Patricia. "It's really like playing detective."

"Yeah," said Learner. "The players are given a minimum of clues, and are allowed to ask questions that will be answered either 'yes' or 'no.' Mr. Hunter knows this one. A man walks into a bar and walks up to the bartender. The bartender points a gun at him, then puts the gun down on the bar. The bartender then gives the man a glass of water. That's it. What's the situation?"

"I hate these things," said DiSalvo, in a grouchy voice.

"Oh, come on, Lieutenant," said Patricia. "Did the man know the bartender?"

"No," said Learner.

"Was it a hold-up?" asked DiSalvo.

"Why would the bartender give him a glass of water if a robbery was taking place? The answer is no," said Learner.

"OK, OK," said DiSalvo. "Was the gun a water pistol and the glass of water was needed to fill it up?"

"Imaginative, but still wrong," said Learner.

"Just give me the answer, will ya' kid?" said DiSalvo.

"The man had the hiccups," said Learner. "The gun was to scare him. When that did not get rid of the hiccups, the bartender tried water."

"Oh, God!" groaned DiSalvo.

"Here's another," said Learner.

"Please!" pleaded DiSalvo.

"Hunter doesn't know this one," said Learner. "A man is running home. He sees a man with a mask. He then runs in the opposite direction. What's the situation?"

"That's it?" asked DiSalvo.

"The way that the game works, Lieutenant," said Patricia, "is that you have to figure out the reality behind the basic clues which ties them together, and makes sense out of seemingly unrelated facts. Those clues can take you in many directions."

Hunter spoke without even looking up from his book.

"It's a baseball game," he said flatly. "The man is running from third base to home plate. He encounters the catcher, wearing the catcher's mask, and runs back to third base."

"Very strong, Hunter," said Learner, "you didn't even have to ask a question."

"Is he always this good?" DiSalvo asked Delvecchio.

"Annoyingly, yes," said Patricia.

"I can't find anything else about those other clues I mentioned," said Hunter. "Getting back to Fisher. I think this murderer would have to know a lot of details about the victims. Where did Wheeler jog? When did Ms. Carlisle ride her horses? When would Dolly Lane be at her beach house? Fisher was not close enough to these people to know all these details. And, as we already pointed out, these deaths have given the children access to immense wealth. That is not something that Reds Fisher would want. He might want to take away, but he would not want to give anything."

"They were also deprived of a computer and a car," offered DiSalvo.

"Small potatoes," said Hunter, "compared to what they will be receiving."

Hunter stopped for a bit to think, and then continued.

"If Fisher is the one," he said, "and you go after him now, without anything definite to implicate him, you may lose him. On the other hand, if the real murderer is setting Fisher up, and you pull Fisher out too fast, the killer will not have his scapegoat, and it's possible that no further attempts may be made to do away with anybody. That may also mean that there will be no more clues to help catch the murderer."

DiSalvo looked at Hunter hard.

"You're asking me to take a dangerous risk," said the lieutenant.

"I know," said Hunter. And then, DiSalvo saw a look on Hunter's face that he had not seen before. It was a cold, rock-hard look, almost frightening. It was the look of a man with a purpose. A man who did not want anything to get in the way of what he was trying to achieve.

"I want this killer," said Hunter. "I want the right person stopped for good."

"OK, OK," said DiSalvo. He hoped the teacher

would cool down. "Let me ask a question, here. You said Gatsby gets killed. How does Myrtle's husband, ah, Wilson, do it?"

"Well," answered Learner, "Wilson shoots him in Gatsby's swimming ... pool."

As the last word was said by Learner, he, Hunter, and Patricia jerked their heads toward each other, their eyes wide open.

"Oh, my," said Patricia faintly.

"The pool!" shouted Hunter.

Then it hit DiSalvo. The Olympic-size pool had just been completed on the EFS campus.

"When's the dedication?" he demanded.

"It's this Friday," said Patricia.

"Do you think," wondered DiSalvo, "that's where the killer will strike next?"

"It could be," said Hunter.

DiSalvo thought for a minute.

"OK," he finally said. "As I said before, we'll keep all of this quiet. Already, too much information has leaked to the press. Practically all of the weird details surrounding Dolly Lane's death have been reported in the media. The fact that the body of a rich woman was found in Atlantic City, a town made for scandal, hasn't helped any. When is the funeral for Dolly Lane taking place?"

"It's this Tuesday," said Patricia.

"I'll be there, with some back-ups," said DiSalvo. "Ditto on Friday at the school. We'll be on the lookout at the wake to see if any attempt is made to steal anything. Hunter, I won't bring in Fisher. But, I'm going to put a tail with some distance on him. And, I guess I'm going to have to start reading literature, again."

He picked up his copy of the novel with one hand. He then looked at the watch on his left wrist.

"It's getting late," he said. "I'll give young James a ride home. Before I leave, I have to use the facilities, Max."

After DiSalvo left the room, Hunter turned to Learner.

"Well, you're still my student for a couple of more weeks," the English teacher said. "And, you have to submit your independent study paper by the end of this week. How's it going?"

Hunter and Learner talked for a few minutes about the paper. A little later, DiSalvo reappeared. As the lieutenant and Learner headed for the door to leave, DiSalvo spoke to Hunter.

"Thanks, Max," he said, "I'll be in touch."

He reached out his right hand to Hunter for a handshake. Hunter took the outstretched hand in his, noted the wrist watch on it, and turned to Patricia.

"So, you persuaded the lieutenant to play, too," he said. "I think the Timex looks better on your left wrist, where it was before."

DiSalvo looked at Delvecchio with a smile.

"You're right," he said. "He is good."

TWENTY-SIX

"SO, WHAT'S THE PROBLEM?" pressed Manny Bergman. He was getting impatient with James Learner's procrastination. It was the Monday after Dolores Lane's death. Finals were coming up, and Learner had not yet delivered on his part of the territory.

"I don't know about this one, Manny," said Learner. He looked around the almost empty EFS parking lot. It was late in the afternoon, and only a few teachers and students were still at the school, taking care of last-minute business.

"I mean, middle school? Isn't the real action in the upper school?" Learner asked.

"Look, I don't want to go through this again," said Manny, obviously trying to control his anger. "The market is there. Pressure gets put on kids to achieve a lot earlier these days."

"Yes, but it's like corrupting minors, selling

them answers to tests, getting them to cheat at that age," said Learner.

"Look," said Manny, reassuringly, "you are not getting them to do anything. They want to do it. Are you afraid you are going to get caught? Don't worry. Some of the actual cheaters might get nailed, but the suppliers don't. The system has been perfected over years. The drop sites and non-student deliverers keep the right people in the dark."

"It isn't about getting caught," said Learner, "it's about right and wrong."

"Oh, so all of a sudden you have a conscience," said Manny sarcastically. "Listen, you are really providing a beneficial service. The system is not fair, man! They keep putting more and more obstacles in a kid's path on his way to the finish line. You're just helping to even things out for some students in this totally rigged race."

Learner had seen too many things go wrong lately, and it all had started to pile up. And, right now he couldn't stand to hear any more of Manny's bullshit.

"Listen," he said, "if all of you put as much effort into the school work as you do into this business, there wouldn't be any need for cheating. I'm out."

He turned and started to walk away.

"Hey," yelled Manny, thinking that guys with consciences could not be trusted, "you're not going to squeal, are you?"

Learner thought for a second.

"No," he said, "I'm just not part of it anymore."

Learner walked to his car, and for the first time in weeks, he felt pretty good.

TWENTY-SEVEN

LT. FRANK DISALVO WAS at the Eastern Men's Athletic Club that same Monday afternoon. He was there to have a one-on-one with Oliver Ford. As he walked through the club, he took note of all the modern equipment and luxurious accommodations. When he arrived at Ford's office, the EFS alumnus was conducting business on the phone. He motioned to DiSalvo to sit down. DiSalvo looked around and saw trophies and photographs of famous athletes, and other memorabilia of the EMAC's past.

Ford hung up.

"What can I do for you, Lieutenant?" he asked.

"Nice place you have here," smiled DiSalvo. "You run it?"

"I have a lot to say about it, yes," Ford smiled back. "But I'm getting more and more involved now with my mother's other real estate activities. But, I don't think you're here to talk about that."

"Well," said DiSalvo, "I know that your security system here is not set up to monitor the movement of every car in and out of the parking lot. So, I know you can't tell me when George Carlisle's car left the day it was stolen, and who was driving it."

He paused.

"Actually," continued the lieutenant, "I have to find out everything I can about the people involved in this investigation. I haven't had a chance to talk with you privately before now. I would like to know what you think about all that has happened, and how you and your mother might be affected."

"You want me to tell you what I think?" asked Ford, an edge to his voice. "Well, I'll tell you what I think. This is a big game, known as the Rat Race. And, those of us who have wealth are the front runners."

"And, somebody is trying to knock you out of the game?" asked DiSalvo.

"Yes," answered Ford, "and whoever it is doesn't care about how many fouls are committed, and isn't afraid of a permanent stay in the penalty box."

He paused. Then he pointed to the windows before continuing.

"All those people out there love this killer. This is a field day for your white and blue collars, and your deadbeats. They are all getting a vicarious, revenge-filled spree, enjoying it every time another one of our parents bites the dust."

"That's a pretty nasty attitude you got there," said DiSalvo. "Do you really think the public enjoys hearing about these tragedies?"

"Enquiring minds want to know," said Ford. "Look, the Founders of this country didn't trust the masses. They wanted the country run by the rich landed gentry, who knew what was best for the country. They didn't want an actual democracy. They knew that would bring chaos. The only thing wrong with our parents was that they were too soft, too generous. It's a different world. Sentimentality has no place if this country is to remain strong."

"And, does this softness also apply to your mother?" asked DiSalvo.

"Yes it does," said Ford. "She is too lenient to those who do not pay their rent on time. I told her to crack down, but she says we have to play along. I told her there's a new game in town."

"About your mother," said DiSalvo, "I've tried to provide security to protect her. She has resisted. She recently said you were against it. Is that true?"

"Having police around is bad for business," said Ford. "People do not feel quite as free to bargain, negotiate. No offense intended, Lieutenant. We have hired some private security people."

"Just the same, I would appreciate it if, at a safe distance, I could provide some protection," said DiSalvo.

"I'll see what I can do," said Ford.

"Well, I'd better be going," said DiSalvo.

"You're welcome to stay as long as you wish," said Ford.

"No thanks," said DiSalvo. "I'm into overtime."

TWENTY-EIGHT

THE LAST COUPLE of weeks of the academic year at most schools are a busy time, and so it was this spring at EFS. Despite the hushed tension that pervaded the halls of the old institution concerning the recent unspeakable events, everyone performed as usual. There were final examinations to take and be graded, papers to be marked, last-minute letters of recommendation for seniors to be completed, and preparations for the graduation ceremony to be made.

For the next two days, Maxwell Hunter allowed himself to be caught up in his work, almost as a mental relief from the other troubling matters in which he had become involved. As he prepared to go to the wake of Dolores Lane on this Tuesday after her death, he recalled the telephone conversation he had had earlier in the day with Lt. DiSalvo.

The lieutenant had told him that the fathers of George Carlisle and Daniel Lane had been located, and both had not been near Philadelphia for some time. Each father had a solid alibi for at least one of the murders. However, the big news was quite unsettling to Hunter. DiSalvo had told him that all attempts to locate Reds Fisher had come up negative. Fisher had requested some vacation time on Monday when he called the hospital where he works. He was not found at his home in Manayunk, and his relatives had not seen him since the news of Dolly Lane's death had been made public. This running away all but damned Fisher in DiSalvo's eyes. The lieutenant had said he would have more time to talk with Hunter at the wake.

Patricia arrived, and she drove both of them to the ceremony. Daniel Lane, unlike his friends, had opted for a small, unpretentious observance for his mother at the well-respected Jordan Funeral Home which catered to the local neighborhood in the Eastwood section. DiSalvo had said he was glad to hear this news, since he could cover the proceedings with fewer officers.

After they entered the attractive Tudor-style

building, Hunter spotted his ex-students. He saw a marked change in their faces. Their eyes darted back and forth, as if on alert. There were forehead wrinkles from worrying. No one smiled. No one spoke. It appears that it has finally caught up with them, thought Hunter. These guys are looking scared.

Hunter and Patricia approached Daniel Lane to offer their respects. Lane had his face down, as if he were hiding it. When he raised it to look at the two teachers, he quickly wiped a tear from his eye.

"Thank you for coming," he whispered to them.

Hunter and Patricia sat down. Mourners filed in. First they approached the coffin, then Lane, and finally the rest of the family. Hunter looked at the floral displays. One was in the form of a clock, to show the time of death. Another was in the shape of a heart, with a red sash in the middle to symbolize bleeding, and the pain of loss.

Time passed. Hunter started to fidget. He loosened his tie. He started to feel claustrophobic. He saw DiSalvo coming out of the funeral director's office. Hunter walked over to the lieutenant. He wanted to get out of there. He had seen too many dead people lately.

"Anything unusual going on?" he asked DiSalvo.

"Nothing. Dull as can be," responded the policeman.

"Anything on Fisher?" asked Hunter.

"Nada," said DiSalvo. "I got a warrant to search his home. I was hoping to find something, maybe information on the victims, maybe Wheeler's computer. I thought it would be nice to find an open copy of *The Great Gatsby*. I got zilch. If he's the one, he cleaned house before he left. We're checking out friends and relatives for any recent contact with him. My guess is that he's holed up in some motel, using an a k a, or, he's long gone. I've been in contact with other police departments to be on the look-out."

Hunter tugged at his tie again.

"I hate wakes," he said.

"There's something I forgot to mention to you on the phone," said DiSalvo. "George Carlisle called us and said that the keys to his Porsche were missing for a short time a few months back. He found them at the Eastern Men's Athletic

Club. He figured someone could have made a duplicate of the keys. I think he figured right."

"Unless," said Hunter, "Carlisle is the killer."

DiSalvo shrugged.

"I think Fisher is our man," he said. "He also belongs to the athletic club, which gave him access."

"Why is he missing, then?" asked Hunter. "He doesn't know that he's been found out, yet. Disappearing would only draw attention to himself."

"Probably a safeguard," said DiSalvo, "just in case someone, as you did, made the Porsche connection."

"Or, maybe," said Hunter, "he figured out that he was being framed, and decided to cut out, buy time, hoping that the real killer would be caught."

"If he suspected something, and he is innocent, he should have come to the police, instead of running away," said DiSalvo. "But, he's bound to show up. He can't hide forever. And that's why I think it would be more prudent, now, since Fisher looks like the one, to beef up security. That means more manpower and metal detectors at the pool ceremony on Friday. I don't have to draw somebody into a trap anymore, and I'd rather not take the chance on another murder taking place."

"If it is Fisher," said Hunter, "he won't know that his plan has been found out if you don't make a big show of force. You may be able to lure the killer into the net, whoever that person may be. Besides, it may not be as easy as you think to find Fisher. If you scare off the killer this time, there are still a lot of families connected with the school, any one of which could be targeted next. The murderer can easily find another pool, at another time."

DiSalvo jammed his hands into his pockets, scraped the floor with one foot, and looked away.

"OK," he said. "But, I'm going to have a bunch of plain-clothes there. There are going to be a lot of alumni at the ceremony who were involved in having the pool constructed. The next victim could easily be one of them."

At that point, Hunter noticed Daniel Lane rise from his seat shakily. He slowly started to walk toward his mother's coffin. As he did so, his right hand reached for his left ring finger, and pulled at it. Hunter slowly moved behind his ex-students. Lane kneeled in front of the casket, and Hunter caught a glimpse of shimmering red and gold.

"What's he doing?" asked Oliver Ford.

"Isn't that his favorite ring?" asked Ronald Wheeler.

"Yeah," said George Carlisle. "It's the gold and ruby one."

"He's giving it back," stated Pierce Bergman.

And, as the young doctor spoke, Lane dropped the precious piece of jewelry into the coffin, quickly rose, and returned to his seat. He then sat down, and held his head in his unadorned hands.

TWENTY-NINE

To the average person, it looked like a lovely, civilized ceremony. It was a beautiful, cloudless, sunny, early June day, this Friday after Dolly Lane's funeral. There were hundreds of smiling people, seated on chairs in front of a raised platform on which stood a lectern with a microphone. The platform was placed in front of the new swimming pool and gymnasium building.

The whole student body and the entire faculty were present. There appeared to be a relaxed attitude among those in attendance, as if those associated with the Eastern Friends School were breathing a sigh of relief that the trying school year was almost over, and that the fun of the summer was about to begin with this party.

But, from where Maxwell Hunter sat, every smile could be hiding a murderous snarl; every move of a hand could lead to danger. The people on the stage, including Dr. Falls and the other school administrators, were possible targets in a gun sight. Hunter hated this feeling. He despised looking at his colleagues, his students, his Quaker school through these desecrated eyes.

He reached for Patricia, who sat next to him, held her hand, and squeezed it. She sensed his need for reassurance.

"DiSalvo has the place covered, I'm sure," she said.

"Right," he croaked.

Hunter paid little attention to the proceedings, as he constantly surveyed the crowd. There was a speech by the athletic director. Dr. Falls then thanked those who had made the addition to the school possible. The headmaster ended by introducing Dr. Thomas Bergman.

"I would like to present one of our most successful graduates," said Dr. Falls, "without whose drive, and generosity, we would not be here today to celebrate this occasion. Dr. Thomas Bergman, would you please say a few words?"

Following a loud ovation, Dr. Bergman began to speak. Hunter noticed that the doctor's family was seated in the front row, which was a couple of rows in front of where he and Patricia sat. And, Pierce Bergman must have invited his friends, since next to Kelly, Manny, and Pierce sat George Carlisle, Oliver Ford, Ronald Wheeler, and Daniel Lane. Seated next to them, Hunter recognized Oliver Ford's mother, Martha Ford.

As he viewed the surroundings, Hunter listened to the conclusion of Dr. Bergman's speech.

"…And it is true that giving is better than receiving. This school has given so much to me and my two sons. It seems only fitting that I, and other alumni, should return the favor, and become the givers. I hope this addition helps EFS to participate in the ancient Greek pursuit of a sound mind in a sound body."

Following the speech, the people on the platform walked to the entrance of the new building, where a long green ribbon spanned the doors. Dr. Bergman was handed a huge pair of gold-colored scissors. Amid people with conventional and video cameras, the doctor cut the ribbon, and everyone applauded.

Hunter looked to his right and saw a man sitting several seats away in the same aisle as the English teacher. Hunter did not recognize him. He saw the man reach into his sports jacket pocket, and start to pull something out. Hunter snapped to attention, and started to rise from his chair, ready to run toward the man. Patricia looked at Hunter in alarm, and grabbed his sleeve. As Hunter stood in front of Patricia, he saw that the man had pulled out a handkerchief. He started to wipe his forehead. Hunter slowly relaxed, felt foolish, and sank back in his chair.

"Are you OK?" asked Patricia.

"No," said Hunter, "not at all."

Dr. Falls returned to the microphone and spoke to the audience.

"Everyone present is invited to walk through the new facility. In the downstairs gymnasium below the pool area, refreshments are being served. Thank you."

The large crowd started to file into the new building. As Hunter entered with Patricia, he was surprised to see how large the edifice was. The pool itself appeared immense. There were stands on all sides for spectators. The ceiling was very high with multiple skylights. As he walked along the edge of the pool, Hunter heard a commotion a bit farther ahead in the line. There followed some shouting. Hunter ran forward. He saw that a couple of men were holding on to the arms of teacher Mark Henry. Lt. DiSalvo now appeared, just before Hunter reached the scene. One of the men holding on to Henry, obviously a plain-clothes man, spoke to DiSalvo.

"Lieutenant," he said, "we noticed a bulge under his arm. We took a closer look, and I saw the handle of a gun."

DiSalvo reached into Henry's jacket and pulled out an automatic hand gun.

"Hey!" said Henry. "What's the problem? I have a permit for that."

"You better have," said DiSalvo calmly. "Let's take him in, boys."

After DiSalvo finished giving his men instructions, and they escorted Mark Henry to a car to be taken to police headquarters, Hunter confronted DiSalvo outside the new building.

"What's the matter with you and your men?" he said. "Mark Henry is not the only one around here who is carrying a weapon for self-defense. After what's been happening, people are scared. And he has even more of a reason, considering what happened to his nephew."

"My men did what they were supposed to do,"

countered DiSalvo. "They were told to be on the lookout for a person with a firearm."

"Well," said Hunter, "I think they jumped the wrong gun. I doubt that Henry could have known the details of the victims' lives so well as to pull off these crimes. And, I don't think that he would feel any sense of gratification by allowing all this wealth to just pass from the parents to the children."

"I don't think that Henry is our man," said the lieutenant. "But, we have to address all possibilities. This argument of yours about inheritance may not wash. If Fisher is the killer, he may just want to have his ex-classmates deprived of their parents, as he was left without a mother, and may not have given a thought about the acts having monetary consequences. And, if it's Henry, he might just be doing it for revenge against rich people, who can give their children everything that money can buy, while he, and others like him, have had to live, and die, on the outs."

Hunter shook his head.

"This murderer thinks things out. I don't believe that he, or she, hasn't thought about consequences," he said. He paused. "In any event," he continued, "your display of strength may have prevented any further developments."

"Well, let's go back inside and keep an eye on things," said DiSalvo.

They did, staying late, waiting for something to happen. Nothing did.

THIRTY

AND NOTHING REALLY happened in the days leading into the next week, as graduation day approached. Mark Henry's gun permit checked out. There was nothing reported stolen by Daniel Lane. Reds Fisher had not turned up. And nobody else associated with the school had been done away with.

Maxwell Hunter fought off depression. He felt that the killer had been scared away at the pool ceremony, which had been the most opportune time for the murderer to be caught. He started to believe that the guilty person would never be discovered, or at least not until one more person died. His only hope, and fear, was that the murderer would not rest until the plot was played out, and someone was found floating, dead, in a pool somewhere.

The school year, in the meantime, was heading quickly towards its dénouement. Final grades had been submitted. The awards assembly had been held on Wednesday (with a few of DiSalvo's police officers discreetly in attendance), and rehearsals for graduation had been conducted. Hunter always loved these ceremonies, which seemed to him to be more special at a private school. There was a strong feeling of fondness for the school on the part of those students who had been going to EFS since kindergarten. Because there were fewer students than at most public schools, there was more attention paid to the individuals, and their talents. The yearbook devoted a whole page to each graduate. The commencement itself contained performances on musical instruments by the students, and poetry readings from the twelfth graders' own compositions.

The graduation ceremony was a whole school affair, with representatives from each grade level adding something to the event, even if it was just decorating the stage, or escorting the guests. Hunter felt that this Quaker attention to the special nature of each person contributing to the community as a whole was what brought alumni and their parents back each year to renew and rejoice in their individuality.

As Hunter drove to EFS to attend the meeting for worship, and the graduation to follow on this lovely Friday afternoon, he thought about how pleased he was with the academic performance of James Learner. James had done a fine job on his independent-study paper. He had attacked the Gothic theme of surface appearance and hidden reality in American Gothic fiction. He had explored this theme in settings, characters, and plots in many works. He had reached back to discuss its roots in European novels, such as Horace Walpole's *The Castle of Otranto,* and Matthew G. Lewis's *The Monk.* He then shifted his attention to the early American novels, Wieland by Charles Brockden Brown, and *The Monks of Monk Hall,* by George Lippard. He addressed the symbolism of light versus dark in the works of Hawthorne, Melville, and Poe, and updated the analysis of this theme by scrutinizing the novels of Stephen King, and including discussion on modern films, such as *Psycho* and *Halloween.*

It was not only the satisfaction he felt concerning Learner's work that made Hunter feel better at the moment. He was also enjoying riding in his

Volkswagen, which had been resuscitated once more. He had tuned in an oldies station on the radio. He listened to songs that spoke of the sun and ocean to be enjoyed during the months to come. He relaxed to the sounds of the Beach Boys' *California Girls* and the Drifters' *Under the Boardwalk*. The music took him away from the crimes of the present to the innocence of his youth. He remembered a song his mother made up and sang to him when he was a child:

Young Max, be happy,
Young Max, stay free.
Run along the windy beach,
Run near the shiny sea.

He let the feelings of the approaching summer wash over him, as he steered through the Eastwood section, toward the EFS parking lot.

THIRTY-ONE

AFTER GATHERING IN the meetinghouse, following the initial silence, the spoken messages began. Maxwell Hunter felt himself sitting next to Patricia Delvecchio, and he vaguely heard others speaking, but he could not pay attention to what was being said. He felt lost in the preliminary stage of the meeting for worship, known as "centering down." His mind seemed to be trying to free itself of external restraints, and closed-minded ways of looking at things. He felt a craving for overview, hoping that the individual pieces of experience would join and form some discernible general shape of the picture of existence.

It was then that he realized that Patricia had stood up, and was reading from a book:

At the still point of the turning world.
Neither flesh nor fleshless;

Neither from nor towards; at the still
point, there the dance is,
But neither arrest nor movement. And do
not call it fixity,
Where past and future are gathered.
Neither movement from nor towards,
Neither ascent nor decline. Except for
the point, the still point,
There would be no dance, and there is
only the dance.

She paused.

"I think," Patricia said, "that T. S. Eliot could
be describing what is at the heart of the Quaker
meeting for worship. I am an American. I am also
a European. I like to think the meeting contains
the good parts of both of those worlds. In a
modern America, which is too often caught up in
the race for material gain, the meeting is a place
which reminds me of the Old World's practice of
stopping to taste food, look at art, talk to one
another, and not take things too seriously. But, the
meeting also holds in it that American respect
for individuality, which is the cornerstone of
the structure of American society. Here, each

person's silent ideas and expressed thoughts are respected. And, the fact that we share this respect together, at the same time, at the same place, makes each of us part of a community. At the still point, one is all, and all is one."

Patricia sat down. Hunter reached over, and held her hand. There was a brief silence. Two seniors stood up and shook hands. Everyone present then shook hands with those seated nearby, and the meeting for worship ended.

THIRTY-TWO

IT WAS NEARLY DUSK when the graduation commencement ceremony began. Earlier, alumni, parents, and guests had taken their seats in the playing fields behind the upper school building. Hunter and Patricia had circulated through the crowd, greeting visitors, and talking with many people. Hunter had been shaking so many hands, his wrist ached. He ran into Manny Bergman, who seemed to be ecstatic about graduating.

"I hope you enjoy your college years," Hunter said to him. He could not help but notice that the youngest Bergman found a way to flaunt his "things" even in a graduation gown. He wore a diamond and ruby tie clasp, a Rolex watch, and gold cufflinks.

"Yeah," he said, "college should be fun. But, what I'm really looking forward to is starting my own cosmetic surgery practice, someday."

"Well," said Hunter, "one thing at a time."

"Too bad that's the way it is, huh?" responded Manny.

Hunter, while looking around for DiSalvo, noticed that Pierce Bergman's friends were again in attendance, this time for Manny's graduation. Lane, Ford, Wheeler, and Carlisle were all seated together near the front of the visitor's section. Hunter could not, however, locate the lieutenant. He had spoken to him on the telephone, and DiSalvo had assured the English teacher that he would be there, with a couple of plain-clothes men. But, he had said that the school's activities had spread his manpower thin. And, there were a number of post-graduation celebrations that had him worried. He was also tied up with the FBI, which had become involved since the body of Dolly Lane was found in New Jersey.

Hunter sat, as usual, next to Patricia, as "Pomp and Circumstance" was being played, and the graduates entered the area in front of the stage. After each student had reached his or her seat, the invocation was read. There followed speeches by Dr. Falls and members of the School Committee of the local Friends meeting. The proceedings were broken up with music performances and poetry readings. The valedictory was given, and, the last song presented before the closing was Crosby, Stills, Nash, and Young's *Teach Your Children,* performed by three graduating seniors on acoustic guitars.

After the students marched out, everyone started to mingle, and there was quite a commotion. Patricia was led away by some celebrating parents. Hunter looked over the happy crowd of faces. He saw James Learner, and worked his way through the crowd toward him. When he reached his now ex-student, all decked out in cap and gown, he patted him on the back and shook his hand.

"Congratulations, James," Hunter said. "I'm going to miss you next year."

"Oh no you won't," said Learner. "I'll come back for some free help on my literature courses."

They laughed and talked for a little while. The songs Hunter had just heard at the ceremony began to fill his mind, and they brought him back to his mother's song. He heard her words in his head:

Run along the windy beach
Run near the shiny sea.

And then suddenly, other lines came to him, lines from a poem:

It was many and many a year ago,
In a kingdom by the sea,
That a maiden there lived whom you may
know
By the name of ANNABEL LEE.

More lines of the poem started to load themselves into Hunter's memory:

That the wind came out of the cloud by
night,
Chilling and killing my ANNABEL LEE.

Hunter quickly turned to Learner.

"James!" he said excitedly. "'ANNABEL LEE' by Edgar Allan Poe. Dolores Lane's middle name was Lee. And, she lived, and died, by the sea."

Realization pulled Learner's eyes wide open.

"Do you remember what Ms. Delvecchio said when we were playing 'Situations'?" asked Hunter. "The clues can mean that something totally different is happening than what appears to be going on. Another author's works have been used as clues in these crimes. Those of Edgar Allan Poe. Remember the doll in George Wheeler's car? It was a Pluto doll."

Learner had just been studying Gothic fiction, so, it did not take him too long to put it together now.

"It's the cat!" he said. "Pluto is the name of the cat in Poe's 'The Black Cat.'"

"Right," said Hunter triumphantly. "And the black ashes on Wheeler's face can also refer to the cat in Poe's story. What about the candlestick found in Dolly Lane's hands?"

Leaner thought for an instant, and then smiled.

"'The Imp of the Perverse.'" he said. "The narrator said he killed his victim by having him inhale deadly fumes from poisoned candlesticks."

"Exactly!" said Hunter. "And, Dolly Lane's death was connected to breathing, since she was smothered. Let me think for a second."

Hunter thought about other details that had

been nagging at him. Sights and sounds played back through Hunter's mind, like videotape being scanned on a VCR. Then, Hunter remembered the awkward words of Pierce Bergman to Reds Fisher at Betsy Carlisle's funeral. Hunter now said the words out loud:

"Don't wait for the pendulum to swing your way."

"What?" asked Learner.

"That's what Pierce Bergman said to Reds Fisher," said Hunter, in a distracted manner. "Wait a second. What about that broken watch that was found on Betsy Carlisle's chest? Also, her throat was slit. These things could have been done to imply that her life on earth was cut short. She was found in a ditch. It all fits."

Learner had been listening intently, and he nodded his head knowingly.

"'The Pit and the Pendulum,'" he said. "The person telling the story is imprisoned by the Spanish Inquisition. He is tied down in a cell that contains a hole which symbolizes the abyss of hell. He sees a picture on the ceiling of Time, with a sharp, swinging descending pendulum replacing the picture of the scythe."

Hunter shivered as he again felt a cold, tingling feeling going up his spine. He pictured in his mind the test booklets of his ex-students. He remembered how Pierce Bergman had written so knowingly about Poe. And then, Hunter had one more revelation.

"Pierce Bergman wrote in blue ink," he said to Learner, "but, he always used a felt-tip pen. The dollar sign in the EFS yearbook found in George Wheeler's lap was written in green ink. But, it was not done by Fisher's standard ball-point pen. A pen with a felt tip had been used."

THIRTY-THREE

QUICKLY, HUNTER LOOKED around, craning his neck, scanning for Pierce Bergman. He could not find him. He did not see DiSalvo, either. Hunter spotted Manny Bergman. He told Learner to wait for him, and Hunter went through the crowd, sometimes shoving not so politely, until he reached Manny. The recent graduate had his arm around a girl, and was talking to her intimately.

"Manny," said Hunter, "please tell me, where is your brother?"

Manny Bergman was obviously not happy with this intrusion on the prelude to one of his romantic conquests, and looked annoyed.

"Oh, I don't know, Mr. Hunter," he said, still holding and looking at the girl. "He went over that way, with my father," he said, and vaguely pointed to a spot beyond the main building.

"Manny!" said Hunter, in a more commanding tone. "Can you please be a little more specific."

The young Bergman turned to face him.

"OK, OK," he said to Hunter. "They went over there, behind the upper school."

And, as Manny spoke, he stretched out his hand and pointed toward the building housing the new swimming pool. Hunter looked in that direction, and then his eyes glided back over Manny's outstretched hand. The cuff of the student's hand was exposed. Then, Hunter saw it, and froze. Manny Bergman no longer wore a gold cufflink on his wrist. It had been replaced with a smooth-surfaced, white one.

"Manny," said Hunter slowly, with a hesitant smile, "that's an interesting, and very attractive, cufflink. What's it made out of?"

Manny smiled, relinquished the female, and showed both wrists to Hunter.

"You like these?" he asked. "They're ivory, in gold settings. Pierce just gave them to me at the end of the ceremony. He wanted me to try them on, to see how they would look with the cap and gown."

Hunter stared, and then shuddered. He knew

those shapes, the contours, the ridges. They were slightly modified, but Hunter knew those cufflinks were made from teeth, just as were those of Meyer Wolfsheim in *The Great Gatsby*. Only, Manny's cufflinks were made from Betsy Carlisle's teeth.

Hunter swallowed, and then backed away without speaking. He found himself heading for the pool, while at the same time he looked for DiSalvo. He saw Patricia and called to her. She ran to him.

"Max, I have to tell you something I just heard," she said. But, before she could continue, Hunter interrupted her.

"Don't ask any questions. Just do what I say," he said. "Call 9-1-1, and ask for more policemen to come here right away. Tell them to go to the pool building. Find DiSalvo, and tell him to meet me at the pool. Dr. Thomas Bergman may be in danger."

To her credit, Delvecchio immediately left to carry out her duties. While he was speaking to Patricia, Hunter noticed a tall, muscular young man with dark hair, glasses, and a beard, who was looking at Hunter and Patricia. When Hunter had finished giving his instructions, the man turned sideways, and looked away. But,

Hunter noticed something unusual about the man's right hand. The fingers were continually being tightened into a fist, and then being relaxed, and then tightened again. Hunter looked closer at the face behind the hair, beard, and glasses. Then he remembered seeing that hand motion at tests he had given, and at EFS sporting events, a number of years ago. He realized that he was looking at Reds Fisher, in disguise, who was drawing on the dramatic talents he had developed so well while he attended EFS. Hunter walked deliberately toward Fisher, and spoke in a low voice when he was close behind him.

"Reds," he said, "it's OK. I need your help." Next to Fisher's ear, he said, "Pierce Bergman is the killer. We have to stop him. He's at the pool."

Fisher turned to Hunter.

"How do you know it's him?" he asked.

"It's a long story, and I don't have time…" Hunter started to say.

But Fisher asked again, urgently, "Tell me what you saw that made you know for sure?"

Hunter hesitated slightly, but sensed that Fisher might know what he was talking about.

"Pierce told you at the Carlisle funeral that he would lend you a tie clasp he had made. So, he makes jewelry," he said. "He gave his brother ivory cufflinks. The cufflinks look like human teeth."

"I understand," said Fisher, quickly. "Let's go."

As they started to run toward the pool, Hunter saw Mark Henry, and called to him.

"Mark!" he said, "do you have your gun with you?"

"Yeah," said Henry, looking defensive, "what of it?"

"We need your help," said Hunter, and he quickly told Henry about Pierce Bergman. As they ran together toward the building, Hunter spoke to Henry.

"Do you know how to use that gun?" he asked.

"I took some lessons," said Henry, "but, I never shot at anyone before, and nobody has ever shot at me."

"I'm afraid," said Hunter, "you may be getting some practice in both of those areas."

They reached the outside of the pool building. The doors were locked, but each faculty member had been given a set of keys to the new building.

Hunter assumed that Thomas Bergman also had a set, and that he and his son were already inside.

"Do you have a plan?" asked Henry.

"Not really," said Hunter, trying to think of a way to avoid the almost inevitable violence that was to come.

"Well," said Henry, "if we get inside without being seen, we can sneak up on him from behind the bleachers."

"I suggest," said Fisher, "that Mr. Henry say that we are the police. That might make him stop and think before shooting."

"I don't think so," said Hunter, doubtfully. "This guy is a proven psychotic killer. You better be prepared to shoot, Mark, at the first sign of trouble."

Hunter pulled out his key and opened the door to the outer entry way. The three men crouched down. Hunter then pushed the inner door open slowly, and all three crept in, sliding to the right, and going behind the bleachers. Hunter took a peek, and saw the Bergmans close to the far end of the pool. They were near the deep part, where there was a steel high-diving platform. Fisher led the way behind the bleachers. Henry was second, and he was followed by Hunter. As they approached the area where the two doctors stood, Fisher went farther on, to the edge of the bleachers. Henry was at the closest opening to the two men between sections of the stands. They could hear Thomas Bergman's voice.

"I still don't see anything, Pierce," he said. "Where is this crack you found?"

"It's over near the side," said Pierce, "near the ladder leading down to the twelve-foot sign. You'll have to get close to the pool to see it."

The older Bergman walked over to the spot in question, and got down on his knees to look. Henry saw Pierce reach inside his jacket.

"Freeze, Pierce!" said Henry. "It's the police!"

"Yeah, put down the gun!" yelled Hunter, his voice reverberating off of the cavernous tile space that enclosed the pool. But, just as the words had come out of Hunter's mouth, Pierce whipped out a gun, equipped with a silencer, and got off a shot. Pierce had aimed at the place where he thought the last voice came from, and the bullet hit close to where Hunter stood. Thomas Bergman had frozen, not seeming to comprehend what was happening.

"Run to the bleachers, Dr. Bergman!" screamed Henry.

Pierce had started to move quickly toward the steel diving tower, and as he did so, he aimed and fired at his father. The bullet hit Thomas Bergman in the right arm, and the elder doctor let out a scream of pain.

"Run!" yelled Hunter.

Thomas Bergman started to run toward the opening in the bleachers, as he grabbed his bleeding right arm. Henry covered him by getting off two shots that caused Pierce to duck down near the platform. Just as his father was about to reach the opening, Pierce straightened up and appeared ready to shoot again.

At that moment, Hunter saw a blur, a human projectile, as Reds Fisher exploded out of the bleachers right at Pierce. Before the young doctor could fire his gun, Fisher body-slammed him, and the gun went flying out of Pierce's hand. The two ex-classmates crashed into the water, and there was a great deal of thrashing in the pool. Hunter and Henry ran toward the pool. They reached the edge, and saw Fisher pummeling Pierce.

"OK, OK," yelled Hunter. "No more, Reds. No more! It's over. Bring him out."

Fisher had one arm held tightly around Pierce's neck, and could easily have choked him to death. But, he loosened his hold slightly, kicked his feet, and swam with one arm, as he brought Pierce to the edge of the pool. Henry still had his gun out.

"Don't try anything, you hear?" he said to Pierce. "You got me in the mood to use this thing, so you better take care."

But Pierce was too banged up, with a swollen shut eye, broken nose, and the wind quite knocked out of him, to try anything. Hunter went over to Thomas Bergman as his former students emerged from the water. Just then, DiSalvo and two police officers entered, and they took it from there. They took hold of Pierce, officially arrested him, and told him his rights. DiSalvo barked some commands into a walkie-talkie, and ordered an ambulance for Thomas Bergman.

DiSalvo looked at Fisher, whose make-up was starting to peel off.

"Who the hell is that?" asked DiSalvo.

"Lieutenant, Reds Fisher," said Hunter. "The

man you were after has just caught your killer. Say hello to the lieutenant, Reds."

"Hi," said Fisher, and he reached out his hand. DiSalvo shook it. The lieutenant then looked at the wounded Thomas Bergman, the beaten up Pierce Bergman, and Mark Henry with his smoking gun still in his hand.

"Some Quaker graduation," he said to Hunter. "I think I'll pass on next year."

THIRTY-FOUR

It was the Sunday after the graduation. Maxwell Hunter, Patricia Delvecchio, James Learner, and Reds Fisher sat in Lt. Frank DiSalvo's office at Police Headquarters. They had all made repetitive statements to the police department concerning their involvement in the investigation. It was late morning, and DiSalvo had just informed them that Manny Bergman's cufflinks did contain teeth that matched Betsy Carlisle's dental records. They were relaxing now, sipping coffee, and eating donuts. Except for Hunter, whom DiSalvo noticed was preoccupied. Hunter stared out the window, drummed his fingertips on the arm of his chair, and seemed to be unable to unwind. Everyone else was listening to Fisher, who had been tied up with the police, and had not had a chance to tell the EFS people his story.

"When did you figure out that you were being set up, Reds?" asked Patricia.

"When I heard about the Porsche and the grocery bag involved in Mrs. Lane's death," he replied, "I became very suspicious. But, I received an anonymous phone call shortly after hearing about the murder of Daniel Lane's mother. It was from someone who said he had gone to school with me, who now worked for the police department, wanted to protect his job, but also wanted to warn me. I didn't trust him, but I listened to what he had to say. He filled me in on those details of the crimes that referred to *The Great Gatsby*. They seemed to jive with what I had read in the newspapers and heard on the TV and radio. After hanging up, and thinking about it, I realized it could have been the killer who had called, wanting to get me out of sight, so that he could do more killing, and still blame it on me. But, I also knew that if I went to the police, it would be difficult to prove my innocence, and the real killer might never be caught. So, I went along with the scheme, hoping I could do more good in hiding. Apparently, I was right."

"How did you know that the next murder

would be at the graduation ceremony?" asked Learner.

"I didn't," said Fisher. "I guessed that a pool might be involved, as did the rest of you. I was at the pool dedication, also, in a different disguise. Only, nobody discovered me that time. I was also at the Awards Assembly. I just wasn't noticed previously."

Fisher paused. Then he continued, with his head lowered.

"I have to confess," he said, "that I felt some satisfaction at first, when the murders happened. These people never knew what it was like to be an average person, *having* to strive, work hard, and squeeze every drop out of what you had to get by. They already had everything money could buy. I was glad to see them hurt, by losing their parents, as I had. I'm sorry, but I did have those thoughts."

DiSalvo walked over to Fisher, and patted him on the back.

"It's alright," he said. "Hell, if I were convicted for all the bad thoughts I had about people, especially in my line of work, I'd be waiting on death row, or sentenced to a hundred life terms. The important thing is, you didn't act on those thoughts."

"By the way," said Patricia, "what I had wanted to tell Max at the graduation before he ordered me to call the police was that I had been talking to Thomas Bergman, just before Pierce led him away. I was trying to get any information about the pool that I could, and Bergman told me to keep a secret. He said it was really Pierce who had suggested that the pool be built, but he thought it would look good for his father to take the credit for the idea. Pierce had obviously been planning a while in advance." She paused. "Lieutenant, how is Thomas Bergman?"

"Not too bad," said DiSalvo. "But he won't be performing any surgery for some time, if ever. His right hand sustained some nerve damage. It will probably allow him to concentrate on his public relations skills."

DiSalvo looked over at the glum Hunter. The lieutenant was in the mood to celebrate, and the English teacher was raining on his parade.

"Damn it, Hunter!" he said, "Lighten up. You did it. You figured it out. The killer is behind bars, bail denied, and awaiting trial. What's the problem?"

"Oh, I'm sorry Lieutenant," said Hunter, with

a forced smile. "You're right. He's been caught. It's just that I don't like the feel of it all. What did you find after searching Pierce Bergman's place at the shore?"

"We found Ronald Wheeler's laptop computer," said DiSalvo. "You'll never guess where it was…"

"Concealed at the bottom of a large doctor's bag," said Hunter.

"Why, yes," said the lieutenant. "How did you know that?"

"I have been going over a few things in my head," said Hunter, "and I recalled that Pierce was carrying a rather large bag at the Wheeler funeral. He must have stolen it that day."

"And," said Fisher, "I'm sure it would have been planted to implicate me, at the athletic club, where I work, in my car, or some other place associated with me."

Everyone nodded their heads in agreement.

"We also found a large number of videocassettes, and audiocassettes," said DiSalvo. "Many of them were of Bergman's friends and his family. But, he apparently liked taping anybody. He had an elaborate, hidden surveillance system installed at his home at the seashore. State-of-the-art. I looked at some of it. Pretty creepy, spying on people like that. The guy is a real loony."

Hunter shook his head.

"I don't like this," he said.

"What's with you?" asked DiSalvo. "We've got it all, haven't we? He knew where Wheeler jogged. It was early in the morning, and he was able to get close to him, since he knew him. He was probably pretending to jog, knocked Wheeler out, and killed him. If someone had been around, Bergman would have asked Wheeler to drive him back to Pierce's car, and he could have done the deed there. Or, he could have waited for another day. Right?"

"Right," said Hunter.

"It was easy to off the Carlisle woman. He knew what she did on the weekends. It was fairly remote where she did her riding. It would have been easy to get in, and out, without being seen. Yes?"

"Yes," replied Hunter.

"And, the Lane killing," continued DiSalvo. "Pierce had stolen the key to Carlisle's Porsche, and had made a duplicate. Then, he made it look

as if the key had been misplaced. But, it was done
at the athletic club, to implicate Fisher. He steals
the car, and parks it in a garage nearby, so that he
can get to it later. He probably temporarily
changes the license plates, so it won't be so easily
detected after it was reported stolen. He's
supposed to be working a night shift at the
hospital. An alibi, but not an air-tight one, since
he can't be accounted for the entire time. He
drives to Dolly Lane's place, and kills her early
the next morning. He then drives to Atlantic City,
and messes up the car to make it seem, again, that
it was done by someone who was anti-rich. He
then takes the train or bus back to Philadelphia."

The lieutenant paused, before continuing.

"We know that he set it up to make it look as
if Fisher was out for revenge. And, he got his
friends inherited wealth, too. He would be able to
use his influence on them, and make deals
quicker, and more to his satisfaction. Even in
Pierce's own situation, Learner told us how Pop
Bergman takes care of all the financial affairs.
With him out of the way, Pierce would have total
control over the family wealth. And, besides,
Pierce Bergman has not denied any of this under

questioning, although he hasn't confirmed any of it, either."

"Oh, it's all true," said Hunter. "But, Pierce wouldn't deny any of it, because he knew you could work all of this out, given the information available. He hasn't given you anything you didn't already know, or couldn't figure out."

"What are you getting at, Max?" asked DiSalvo.

"We know why Pierce made references to Gatsby at the scenes of the crimes," said Hunter, "but, why did he leave clues having to do with the works of Edgar Allan Poe? Why did he give those cufflinks to Manny?"

"I don't know," said DiSalvo. "He's a psychopath. Who knows why crazy people do crazy things."

Just then, there was a knock at the door. DiSalvo opened it, and let in a stout man, who wore large horn-rimmed glasses.

"Everyone," said DiSalvo, "this is Dr. Fowler. He is the Bergmans' psychiatrist. The family wanted him to talk to Pierce while he was being held here, pending transfer to a maximum security prison. Is there anything I can do for you, Dr. Fowler?"

"Yes," said the psychiatrist. "I was told by your sergeant that an English teacher, by the name of Maxwell Hunter, was here."

"Yes," said Hunter, "I'm Maxwell Hunter."

"I've just been speaking with Pierce," he said, "and, without divulging anything which would compromise doctor-patient confidentiality, I have to tell you that Bergman frightens me. I am telling you this, because he asked me to give you a message, and a request."

"What is this?" demanded DiSalvo.

"No," said Hunter. "Go on, Dr. Fowler."

"Pierce said," relayed the doctor, "'How do you think you did in the test, Mr. English? Come and see me for your final grade.'"

"This is nuts," said DiSalvo. "Hunter, you don't have to see him."

Hunter turned to the lieutenant.

"Yes, I do," said Hunter. "You see, he's had me in mind the whole time."

THIRTY-FIVE

MAXWELL HUNTER WAS escorted by two uniformed policemen and Lt. DiSalvo to a sub-floor below the police headquarters' lobby. It was here where physical evidence was held, and prisoners were temporarily incarcerated. And, it was here where Pierce Bergman currently was imprisoned.

After getting off the elevator at the third sub-level, they passed through several security checkpoints stationed next to steel bars which divided the floor into many parts. There were heavily armed police officers everywhere, and the entire area was under electronic surveillance. As they walked down a white corridor, they came to a steel door.

"He's in a cell on the other side of the door," said DiSalvo. "There's a small reception area in front of the cell. There is a button on the side of the chair in the reception area, which you can push to signal that the meeting is at an end, or to indicate any problem. The door will be immediately opened by officers on guard outside."

DiSalvo paused.

"Are you sure you want to do this?" asked the lieutenant.

"Yes, I'm sure," said Hunter. But DiSalvo doubted it.

"OK," said DiSalvo, "see you in a little while."

As he entered, Hunter saw Pierce Bergman's back. He was behind two rows of steel bars placed in an alternating fashion. This made it impossible for the inmate to reach out to the other side. There was a small rectangular opening at the bottom of the cell, which was covered by a rectangular sheet of steel, and which appeared to be locked. Hunter assumed that food on a tray could slide through it. There was a bed affixed to the wall, and a sink with paper cups sitting on its edge. There were two face cloths hanging over the sink, and there was a toilet next to the sink.

"Please," said Bergman, "have a seat, Mr. Hunter, sir."

Hunter looked at Pierce's back, and slowly sat down on the only chair in the room, which was secured to the ground. There was also a small table, also bolted to the floor, in front of the chair. Bergman slowly turned around. What Hunter saw after Bergman had completed the rotation was a face that looked like a Halloween mask.

Fisher's beating had caused Bergman's left eye to swell almost shut. Black colored the skin around the eye. The nose was also badly swollen due to the breakage, and one nostril had been packed. He had also obviously sustained a few hard blows to the left ear, because it, too, was quite enlarged. But, the most disgusting sight was Bergman's mouth. Pierce maintained a steady, unnerving grin, which revealed severely bruised, oversized lips, and the loss of his two upper front teeth.

"So nice of you to visit me," said Bergman, his voice almost a hiss. "So, what do your friends think of all of this?"

"They think," said Hunter, staying steady, keeping eye contact with the creature in front of him, "that you did it to have your friends inherit wealth, and so that you could control your family's money."

"What else?" Bergman grinned.

"And that you set up Reds Fisher to take the blame, thereby getting back at someone you very much disliked since your high school days."

"Well," said Bergman, "those certainly were a few of the birds to be killed by the same stone."

Bergman's hideous smile widened.

"And," Hunter's ex-student said, "what do you think?"

Hunter leaned forward, placing his elbows on the table in front of him.

"I thought about the two elements present in each death," said Hunter. "On the one hand, something was given—wealth. And, on the other hand, something was taken away—a parent. A thing and a human being. One would normally think that was a contradictory action, helping and hurting the receiver at the same time."

Hunter paused, and put his hands together.

"But, I started to think about you, Pierce. What you were like in high school. How much you enjoyed science, dissecting animals, looking at specimens under the microscope, trying to see what made living things tick. You were a dispassionate observer, and you looked at people as others would look at guinea pigs in a large laboratory. Just now, Lt. DiSalvo told me you had a large number of tape recordings of your friends. It appears that you haven't changed."

Hunter took a breath.

"I think this was one big experiment, Pierce. You were giving those you could observe tangible wealth, and were removing representatives of intangible love. You wanted to see how they would respond, what they cared for more. You even included your brother in the experiment, since Manny's reaction to your father's death would be easy for you to measure. The stolen computer and Porsche were used not just to implicate Fisher, but also as instruments to measure the intensity of feelings for possessions versus people. I suspect Daniel Lane's ring was to be the next item to disappear, and be used in the Pierce Bergman Sentimentality Test."

"Yes," hissed Bergman, "a test Daniel, alas, had too much heart to pass. Mr. Hunter, you will be able to read my analysis, since I intend to publish the results of my study. Which, I am sure, the media will love to get their hands on, given my current state of notoriety. Of course, even if I had not been caught, there would have been much interest in my insider's view on those involved in the recent events. I bet you didn't think that would be one of the birds killed with the same stone. That I would become famous."

"No," said Hunter, realizing more and more with what he was dealing. "I didn't."

"Oh, but you're doing quite well, Mr. Quaker school teacher," said Bergman. "I'll be sure to send you a copy of my study on human behavior for Christmas. Autographed, of course." He paused. "Anything else you'd like to add?"

"Yes," said Hunter. "I know you wanted me involved in the investigation. You counted on my passion for mystery-solving, added to my familiarity with the people involved. It's easy to see how my knowledge about Robert Fisher's fascination with *The Great Gatsby* would help point the finger of guilt at him."

Hunter rose from his seat and started to pace the small room, while Bergman remained perfectly still.

"But, why the references to Edgar Allan Poe?" asked Hunter. "They served no purpose in the practical scheme to transfer wealth and implicate Fisher. And giving Manny those cufflinks certainly wasn't going to help you obtain those objectives."

Hunter paused, and then continued.

"But, the candlestick in Dolly Lane's hand kept reminding me of Poe's *Imp of the Perverse*. Just as the murderer in that tale could not hold his tongue about the crime he had committed, just as the killer in *The Black Cat* felt compelled to tap, in front of the police, on the wall behind which was placed his victim, so, you, too, had to announce your deeds in an extra set of clues."

"Well, you have to admit," said Bergman, "that to play the lead in such wickedly deceptive crimes, and not be allowed to take a curtain call, would be very frustrating. Of course, if you had not found me out, I still would have delighted in tricking you. By the way, how did you hook into the Poe angle?"

Bergman's stare was calm, detached, as if they were discussing a paper written for a class.

"Just lucky," said Hunter. "A student had done independent study on Gothic fiction. My mind had been sensitized to the area, and I clued in."

Hunter paused, and looked coldly into the distorted, smiling face.

"Of course," he continued, "since you used a felt-tip pen to draw the dollar mark in the yearbook, and not Fisher's standard ball-point pen, I naturally suspected you."

Bergman said nothing, but there was a momentary tremor in the smile, and, Hunter knew he had scored a point. Pierce had made a mistake with the pen, and did not realize it until now.

"You certainly performed well on this specific exercise," said Bergman, "and I am forced to give you an 'A'. But, I don't think you have truly learned the lesson."

Bergman stopped talking, and slowly approached the bars, his smile now becoming a grimace.

"Perverseness," Bergman said, "according to Poe, is that aspect of human nature which makes us act in a certain way, for the very reason we should not. One commits a vile deed because that person should not do so. We violate that which is law, merely because we understand it to be such. Everything has its underside, the desire to hurt and be self-destructive. Each thing has its ugly side. Even the Catholic Church, in the form of the Spanish Inquisition, whose cruelties in the dungeons are depicted by Poe in *The Pit and the Pendulum.*"

Hunter sat down again as he listened to his former student's lecture.

"I recognize the imp of the perverse in me," said Bergman, "and in the world at large. You do not."

Bergman then pointed to his own face, and continued talking.

"This is the face underneath the facade of all those proper daily activities. This is the reality of today, in all levels of our society. You, Mr. Sixties Man, are obsolete. A fraud. An anachronism. Do you really know many people who are like you? Do you really have many friends who believe as you do? Who believe in the brotherhood of humankind? That laws and government can cure all ills? Do you know anybody who reached the mountain top, and had realized a dream about how wonderful the future will be? Do you even know anyone who thinks or cares about the future? I suspect you really are a lonely man."

Bergman stopped, turned around, started to walk away, then did an about-face, and approached the bars again.

"Oh, one more thing," he said. "I'll be back, you know. My parents will spare no expense for lawyers, psychiatrists, political clout. Do you want to know why they will help me, even though I tried to kill my father?"

"I would think, Pierce," said Hunter, "that despite what you are, that your parents still see you as their son, and that they love you."

"Ha!" exploded the laugh from Bergman's mouth. "You really don't get it, do you? Nobody is listening to us, because there is no need. They have the guilty person. So here it is. Tell me Mr. Mystery-solver, did you ever see my mother drive a car?"

"No," answered Hunter, "I don't think so."

"Well," Bergman said, "she's quite careless. In fact, she's very careless about a lot of things. She was careless the night that Reds Fisher's mother was killed."

Hunter felt himself beginning to sweat.

"It was my mother," continued Bergman, "who was driving the Porsche that killed that woman. My mother was having an affair with the owner of the car. He lived in the Eastwood area. They had a fight. They had had too much to drink. She sped off in his car, and ran over Mrs. Fisher. Oh, they did an exquisite cover-up. They bribed the right people, and pinned it on some poor ex-con. Of course they had to keep it from the boys. However, I had already become quite adept at spying on people. If I had been successful at doing away with my father, I would have blackmailed my mother to make sure I had control of the family fortune. Since things have turned out this way, I can blackmail them both. Again, you must kill as many birds as you can with the stone you are provided."

The sick smile was back in full force.

"My parents will never get caught without my help. Even if you tell DiSalvo, you won't find any evidence out there anymore."

"You know I'll tell him," said Hunter, breathing quickly. "He'll find a way."

"No," said Bergman. He started to laugh. "I'll be back, Hunter, oh, I'll be back." He paused. "Your Quaker friends only tell you half the truth. They say there is a part of God in everyone. What they don't want to admit is that there is a part of the devil in each of us as well."

Hunter pressed the button on the chair repeatedly. He wanted to get out of there, fast.

"I'll be back," Bergman repeated.

The outer door opened, and the guards entered. As Hunter sprang for the doorway, he heard Pierce Bergman calling after him.

"I'll be back," he said. "I'll be back, Hunter, because I am the future."

THIRTY-SIX

LT. FRANK DISALVO escorted Maxwell Hunter and Patricia Delvecchio through the entrance doors of the police headquarters, and down the front steps. DiSalvo had already told them that Reds Fisher had given James Learner a ride home. Hunter had related what Pierce Bergman had said about the death of Robert Fisher's mother.

"Do you think you'll be able to turn up anything on Mr. and Mrs. Bergman?" asked Patricia.

"It's been a long time," said DiSalvo. "But, I'm a hard worker, and I'll keep looking until something turns up. If bribes were involved, I won't quit until I find the people involved."

"Don't work too hard," said Hunter. "In fact, I think you should take a vacation, first. Get away for awhile."

"Hm," muttered DiSalvo, "that's not a bad idea.

I'd like to go to the seashore a bit, under more enjoyable circumstances than those on my recent trip."

"Keep in touch," said Hunter. "I think that's the first time I ever said that to a cop."

"Well, then, I guess you've learned something from all of this," said DiSalvo.

"More than I ever wanted to," said Hunter, softly.

"Well, thank you again, and I'll see you both at the trial," said the lieutenant. He shook their hands and turned to go back into the building. Hunter and Patricia started to walk toward the Peugeot.

"I think I had better practice what I preach," said Hunter. "Can you still get tickets for that trip to Europe?"

"I know a travel agent who can book us on a flight very quickly," said Delvecchio. "When would you like to leave?"

Hunter gazed at the city's skyline, which looked like a cut-out pasted against the gray, overcast sky. He stared at the statue of William Penn, the Quaker founder of Pennsylvania, perched atop City Hall, which looked over the City of Brotherly Love.

"The sooner the better," said Hunter.

As they walked, they saw the flashing light of a police car in the distance as it approached, its siren getting louder.